HUNGRY FOR YOU

© 2011 A.M. Harte
ISBN 978-1926959290

Cover art design: MCM
Book design: Tim Sevenhuysen

1889
LABS
Published by 1889 Labs Ltd.
Visit our website for free books and other fun stuff:
http://1889.ca

A LOVE TO DIE FOR

by Gabriel Gadfly

Darling,
In the event of a zombie apocalypse,
I'm gonna marry you.
And I know that romantic testimonial
isn't quite the matrimonial proposition
you were expecting,
but I'm projecting a lovely future for us.
You see,
when the dead break free,
I'll come save you.
I'll be your knight in shining Kevlar,
your cranium-crushing crusader,
and safe in our barricaded bungalow,
we'll match moans for groans
with the shambling horde outside.
We'll make love 'til death do we part,
or at least 'til we start
to run out of supplies,
and if we get in a pinch,
I've got a surprise:
see, I'll paralyze them with poetry,
'cause if there's anything a zombie understands,
it's desire.

Meanwhile,

you lay down suppressive fire

and we'll take out as many as we can.

And if in the end

we are overrun,

I'll let them take me

so you can get away.

They can have my brain—

it's my heart that beats for you.

TABLE OF CONTENTS

HUNGRY FOR YOU

A.M. HARTE

Anna Harte

resisting their basic impulses.

"Maybe he's gay," Mort said, edging away from the bed.

But the zombie didn't track Mort's movements, didn't react as he had with Retta. She crouched down to get a better look at the zombie. His skin was dark brown and stretched thin but he was hardly decayed; she could still see the vestiges of what must have been masculine beauty in his dark floppy hair and square jaw line.

"Ten fingers and ten toes," Mort remarked. "This guy sure's been lucky."

Too lucky. Who knew how long he'd been tied up? Over a day at least, judging by the indentations the rope had left on his wrists. How had he fed in that time, unless—? She glanced down to his lower body and found the expected signs.

"He was raped." Retta nodded to herself. "Repeatedly. There's no other explanation. He's so overstuffed he can't even face looking at another morsel—that is, me."

Mort shook his head. "A man can't never have too much food, Sarge. 'Sides, does it even count as rape?"

She frowned. "Why shouldn't it? Because he's a prostitute? A zombie?"

"Either." Mort shrugged. "Both."

Retta bristled. "You know he didn't have any choice in this. Besides, he's still *human*, Mort. That government report showed they still have feelings. He has rights under the law." Not many, true, but it was better than nothing.

"Maybe he shouldn't." Mort looked away sourly. "Just saying."

The flash of anger was hot and sudden. "And maybe you should lose that attitude."

Mort knew not to push his luck. He walked around the bed to stand by her side. "We done here yet?"

"We can't leave him here," Retta replied. "Whoever did this may come back."

"You wanna take him in? And do what?" Mort placed a hand on her shoulder. "Look Retta, you gotta let this shit go. Your sister and boyfriend were zoobs, so what? They're gone now. Even if they were still alive or whatever, they wouldn't be the same *people* you remembered. You can't spend the rest of your life running after these creatures. Sooner or later they'll die for real. The sooner, the better."

She didn't look at him, didn't even move. Retta kept her eyes on the zombie lying prone on the bed, so helpless. Her voice was cold and hard. "He's been *raped*, Mort. And his restraints do not comply with the 10 yard government regulation. There are procedures to follow."

She felt more than saw Mort shake his head. "And what're you gonna do when he gets hungry again?"

"We'll figure something out." She didn't wait for Mort to protest, just moved closer to the bed. "Now help me get him into the car."

*   *   *

"I hope you know what you're doing, Sergeant Retta," the Chief of Police said, watching Mort lead the zombie to an interrogation room. The zombie shuffled after Mort without putting up any resistance, as docile and compliant as when they'd found him in the house.

"I appreciate you giving me this chance," Retta

replied.

The Chief leaned against the door of her office, looking at her over his glasses. "You should ask Cane for advice," he said.

Retta looked over her notepad, jotting down questions to ask the zombie. "Will do, Chief."

He sighed. "Retta…" Something about the tone of his voice made her look up. He seemed all of a sudden old. "You're a good cop, Retta," he said. "But the sooner you learn to let certain things go, the better for all of us."

She looked at her desk, biting back a sarcastic answer. By the time she looked up the office door was closed and the Chief was gone. With no one there to see her, Retta allowed herself a moment of weakness, letting her shoulders slump heavily. What *was* she doing? What would this prove?

The door began to open and she straightened, looking through the pages on her desk with feigned concentration.

"We're ready for you," said Mort, walking into her office. He had a set of keys in one hand and some paperwork in the other.

She took the paperwork from Mort and scanned it. "John Doe?"

Mort shrugged. "What else could we call it?" He tossed the keys on her desk, then took a bar of chocolate out of his pocket and began to unwrap it. "The zoob's still not hungry, so if you wanna ask questions, you better do it now."

Retta nodded. "I'll come in a second." She waited until Mort had left her office, then picked up the phone and called Cane. As head of the specialised DK9-unit, he supervised the training and deployment of zombie dogs throughout the city. With a zombie's sense of smell, the DK9 dogs had rapidly become a popular choice for drug busting operations, although keeping the dogs well-fed was a challenging task. When he answered the phone, she launched straight into the problem with barely a hello.

"You're the closest we have to a zombie expert on-site," she began. She quickly outlined the zombie's situation, how she'd discovered him and her decision to bring him in. At the end she asked, "So what do you recommend?"

There was a long pause. "I only work with dogs, Retta—"

"But they're zombie dogs! Surely there's some similarity?"

"I guess." Cane didn't sound certain. He paused. "First thing I do with a new dog in need of training is speak to it. Get it used to the sound of my voice. After it starts responding you can move onto more difficult stuff, the important's building that connection first." Loud barking interrupted him. Cane cursed. "Got to go. Bye." The line went dead before Retta could ask another question.

Damn it. Well, she'd just have to do the best she could. Retta took a deep breath and gathered up her paperwork before making her way down the hallway, ignoring the knowing glances the other officers threw her way.

She opened the door of the interrogation room and walked right into the zombie. He just stood there, unresponsive, no doubt standing in the exact spot where Mort had left him. Retta sighed and—with no

followed Mort to the observation room. John was deteriorating quickly: his movements were already more sluggish, his skin growing dull. His head snapped up when they entered the observation room and he began moving towards the one-way mirror, his nostrils flaring. The skin around his eyes had begun to peel.

Retta took a deep breath, thinking quickly. "Maybe he is gay after all. Have you tried him with a male?"

"Tried him with everything. He's got a boner, he's just not using it. At this rate he'll be dead for real in a few days."

"I don't understand." Retta stared through the one-way mirror at John, who was pressed against the glass looking at her—or where his nose told her she was. "Isn't he hungry?"

"'Course he is." Mort took a large bite out of his triple-decker sandwich, chewing with relish. "Thing is," he said, spraying crumbs onto the floor, "he's only hungry for you."

SWIMMING LESSONS

"We'll be safe here," Matt pronounced, his voice trembling with the weight of the last few days. He dropped the guns—useless now, empty of bullets—and stuck his hands in his pockets.

Nathan nodded, focused on filming the small cluster of houses in front of them. After the horror of the mainland, the rotting bodies and the moans of the undead, there was something strangely idyllic about the cheerfully painted cottages, the neatly trimmed grass and the light wisps of clouds in the sky. He almost expected his wife to come running out of the red cottage at the far end wearing one of her white slips hemmed with lace. Nathan zoomed in on the cottage but the doorway stayed closed. His heart felt like lead in his chest.

"Well," Matt said, and his voice was stronger now, "we should relax. God knows it's been ages since I've sat around doing nothing." He threw himself onto the wooden bench, tilted his face up to the sun. "No one else can get onto this island, right?"

"I trashed all the other boats," Nathan replied, turning on the spot to film the panorama. It was a habit that had formed over the last week. His filming had been instinctual at first, an attempt to somehow preserve the world by capturing its ruin. Now it was almost a ritual. "Besides," he added, "there's no one left to fix them."

"Just you and me in paradise, then." Matt shaded his eyes and grinned. "Shame you're not a girl."

Nathan turned off his camera and cocked an eyebrow. "If anyone's the girl, it's *you*."

"Yeah right! I'm the one being stalked by Vicky-the-zombie, remember? Even after death I'm a stud."

How Mark could joke about his now ex-fiancée was a mystery. She'd been chasing them with typical zombie hard-headedness for days, her previous lust and love transformed to hunger. Nathan's wife had done the same, too, until he'd shot her in the head. The memory made his gut clench and he turned away to hide his expression.

Mark noticed. "Sorry, man."

Nathan shook his head. "Whatever." He stared at the red cottage and wished himself back in time, wished desperately and without hope. His nails dug into his palms and red spots danced across his vision but nothing changed.

"It's just weird." Mark's voice was soft, as wispy as the clouds. Nathan stared, raised an eyebrow. "Them chasing us, that is," Mark explained. "All those other people they could've eaten and they came after us instead."

The camera in Nathan's hands creaked, his knuckles turned white. "It's because they know us." Nathan had gone back home and she'd been there waiting as she always had, except it hadn't been her, not anymore. "We're familiar. Everything else has changed and we're all they have left."

He was half-expecting Matt to reply with one of his

usual faux-intelligent comebacks to lighten the mood, but Matt's face had gone pale, his eyes focused on a spot somewhere over Nathan's right shoulder. Matt raised a shaky hand, pointed. "Errr… What's that?"

Nathan turned around, bringing his camera up to bear. He stared through the lens, pressing the zoom button hard. There! By the shoreline. Movement. Something was coming out of the water. Lumbering forward, towards them. Was it—?

Nathan swallowed heavily, lowered his camera, and said, "It looks like Vicky has learned how to swim."

A PRAYER TO GARLIC

"Your mother is going to kill me."

Mog looked up from the dining room table. He had paint on his cheeks and hands, and the little girl beside him was even more of a mess. His smile—more of a sunken grimace ever since his premolars had fallen out—was sheepish. "Well, she always said you'd make a man out of me."

"And I just had to go and prove her right, didn't I?" I shuffled over to the table and sank down into the chair next to Mog and across from the child. The two were a portrait of contrasts, him milky-eyed, pale and wrinkled, the girl all succulent sweetness with long blond pigtails and rosy cheeks.

Mog dipped his finger into the red paint pot before answering. "If it makes you feel any better, it was more this one's doing than yours," he said, nodding at the young girl, who took it as an invitation to speak.

"For you," she said. She pushed her painting towards him. She'd drawn four stick figures of varying sizes, surrounded by flowers—whether those figures were humans or zombies wasn't clear.

Mog looked genuinely delighted. He stroked the little girl's hair. "That's a nice garden you drew," he told her. "Do you want to see our garden? It has the best bone arrangement in the county."

The girl nodded enthusiastically, pushing herself up onto her feet to stand on the chair, toddler legs wobbling. "We go outside?"

"You go first," Mog replied, swinging her down from the chair. He made sure she was steady on her feet, then let her go. "I'll come in five minutes."

"Okay!" The girl hesitated, then unpeeled something long and brown from around her waist: Mog's index finger. "This yours!" She handed it to him, then skipped through the veranda and out into the backyard. The dining room was colder and quieter with her absence; for a moment I wondered how odd we must have looked, sitting so still with only the rhythmic pulsing of our brains marking the passage of time.

But our brains—our healthy, glistening brains— would only keep us alive for so long. The stress of moving an otherwise dead body was already taking its toll; I was six months old and keenly aware that half my life was over. I smoothed out the wrinkles in my left hand, pulling the excess skin down to cover the exposed bone of my pinkie.

When I looked up, Mog was studying his index finger, trying to reattach it with no success. "That'll need stitches," I said sourly. "I told you not to go out into the midday sun." Not that he ever listened.

Mog half-shrugged, scratching his head. "I wanted to surprise you." His ear fell off and landed with a thud on the tabletop. The image of him disintegrating before my eyes made me sick. That I could lose him so easily…

I got up hurriedly, shot him the glare I generally reserved for prey. "Honestly, darling, we've got to eat off of this table." As he mumbled an apology, I took his ear and finger and shuffled over to the kitchen. The freezer was full of chopped up meat, but I found space on the top shelf, squeezed his ear and finger in for safe-keeping. Then I shuffled over to the wall and turned the already blasting air conditioning up a notch.

Mog appeared at the kitchen doorway, holding a piece of paper. He held it out towards me. "For you," he said.

It was the finger painting he'd been working on. Most of the page was blank, but right in the middle, in sharp, exquisite detail, was a human heart. His heart.

Mog touched his chest. "I'm glad we found each other."

"Don't be silly," I retorted, but I folded the drawing very carefully and slipped it into my pocket. "We died next to each other. We didn't have far to look."

"Still," he replied, "I'm glad we're together."

But for how long? I took his hand. Through the kitchen window I could see the little girl squatting down to examine one of the bone sculptures. There were fifteen of them spread throughout the garden, although only fourteen were visible from any one vantage point.

"Her tendons would be perfect for sewing your ear back on, you know."

Mog shook his head. "I can't do it, sweetie. I'm sorry."

I sighed. Neither could I, but it went without saying. Mog had known about my alternative eating habits for months. But it was something we'd hidden from his mother, who was a traditional zombie to the core. She scoffed at the mere suggestion of pork. Not to mention how she'd react whenever she met the chicken-eaters down the road.

"Vegetarians, the lot of them," she'd say. "I survive on human and marrow pie, and if it's good enough for me then it's good enough for them!"

She'd clearly never been in close contact with humans, never had the chance to see that—despite their savage, selfish ways—there was more to them, there was depth.

I rubbed my forehead tiredly. "Your mother's arriving in two hours, and if we don't have dinner on the table, she's going to rip out our arms."

"I still like human meat," Mog said stubbornly. "I just… just can't eat hers." His comment was punctuated by a delighted giggle which drifted in from the garden; the girl had picked up a bone and was drawing shapes in the gravel.

As usual, it would be up to me to clean up the mess. I fished a pork bone out of the pocket of my dress and sucked on it thoughtfully. "Go put the girl back where you snatched her while I think something up."

Mog straightened, his movements slow and lumbering. "What're you going to do?"

"I've got no choice now, do I?" I crunched the bone into small pieces before continuing. "Make a pork pie. And pray the garlic will cover up the difference."

DEAD MAN'S ROSE

The happy illusion of married life lasted less than three days. Alba leaned against the kitchen table, fighting back the tears that would send streaks of mascara down her face to mingle with the growing bruise on her cheek. The kitchen was spotless, perfect; the shining white marble surfaces were a cruel reminder of what her husband was accustomed to, and what she could not offer.

"We can't go on our honeymoon with you looking like this." The disgust in Rick's voice made Alba cringe further into her shoulders.

"Sorry," she said in a small voice that barely broke the silence. She desperately wanted his approval but it was so difficult to please him. "I was only…" Words failed, her tongue thick in her mouth. She twisted her wedding ring nervously. "Nothing happened. He was visiting. We talked about *salsa* so I was showing him the dance steps."

Rick's eyes were cold and hard, frightening. "I'm cancelling the honeymoon," he said as if she had not spoken at all. "I hope you're happy."

"No, please, I…" She reached up to touch her cheek without meaning to, jerked her hand away when his eyes narrowed. "*Por favor*, he is only *un vecino*, the neighbour. It was nothing." She would never cheat on him—couldn't he see that?

The silence lengthened. Rick walked to the doorway, his head turned away as if he could not bear to look at her. "If you can't speak in English, then don't speak at all." He left the kitchen and moments later the front door slammed behind him.

Alba bowed her head, cursed her family and the poverty that had so shaped her, wishing for a moment that Rick had not rescued her from her dead-end life because she was not worthy of his attention. If only she were English and well-off, like the wives of Rick's colleagues…

The rumbling of a car engine cut off her train of thought. He was leaving her! Alba ran to the front door, threw it open to find the car backing out of the driveway. "Wait!" she called. "Wait!" But he ignored her, kept reversing, and soon the car was on the main road and he was driving away, the car getting smaller and smaller until it turned a corner and he was gone.

She sank down onto the front porch, wondering when her husband would return, *if* he would return. What if he wanted her gone? She toyed with the idea of returning home and facing the knowing stares and her mother's never-ending nagging. No: she could not do it. It would be far better if she crawled underneath the front porch, into the dark spaces beneath the house, and never came back.

Alba sat forlornly on the front porch long enough for the spring breeze to work its way through her thin t-shirt. Eventually she began to shiver. She got to her feet, walked back into the house that even now showed no signs of her existence. The austere, expensive furniture was nothing like she had ever owned, and for a moment Alba felt that she was being slowly erased.

She wandered into the living room. Her mobile phone was missing and the house phone line had been cut, but Alba knew better than to leave the house again. She sat down on one of the stiff leather couches in the room and placed her head against her knees. All she could do was wait.

*   *   *

Six hours later, Rick came back.

Alba jumped when she heard the front door open, ran a critical eye across the kitchen surfaces. Everything was clean, the table set for two with napkins folded the way Rick liked them. Dinner—his favourite—was in the oven. Alba smoothed down the front of her dress, patted her hair to make sure it still covered the bruise.

When she looked up, Rick was in the doorway. He examined the room, then took in her dress and heels. "Tuck your hair behind your ear," he instructed, and Alba did, nervous as his eyes lingered on her cheek. But he said nothing.

Rick walked further into the room and it was then Alba noticed the flowers he was carrying, a big bunch of roses with curling petals and crisply ironed leaves, the stems stiff and unbending even in his strong, large hands. For a moment Alba hated the roses for their purity, for deserving his touch when she didn't. Then Rick laid them down onto the table and Alba realised they were for her.

"I didn't want to," he said, "but you made me really angry."

She froze, staring. Was that an apology? When she didn't react, Rick frowned and pointed at the flowers.

"Put them in water."

Alba kept her head down as she gathered up the bouquet, using both arms where he'd used one. Up close the roses were more fragrant than expected, but sharper too, an armful of pleasure and pain.

Rick raised an eyebrow. "Well?"

"They're beautiful," she said. "Thank you."

When she'd finished arranging the flowers in a vase, Rick beckoned. "Come here," he said. There was a little crease in the middle of his forehead.

Had she done something wrong? Alba moved around the kitchen table with a mixture of dread and terrible excitement. Her heart was overheated, running faster than usual, *tha-thump, tha-thump, tha-thump*. The bruise in her cheek throbbed in time to her steps.

She braced herself when he raised his hand but he only pulled her closer, wrapping his long, strong arms around her. His body was hard, stone-like against hers, and Alba wilted into him, felt herself fade as she became part of something greater than herself. He had forgiven her. All of a sudden she was crying.

Rick hushed her, stroked a long, possessive line down her back. The breath was crushed out of her but she didn't dare complain. "My rose," he murmured into her ear. His breath was tinged with bourbon. "My beautiful rose."

Later, when Alba was washing the dishes, she picked up a stainless steel pot and saw the tired face of a stranger in the reflection. A map of reds and purples bloomed along the strange woman's face and Alba found herself wondering how much time would pass before more continents joined the first.

When Rick called her to bed, Alba took one of the

roses from the bouquet he had given her and plucked its petals as she walked upstairs, leaving a trail of red softness behind her. By the time she reached the master bedroom only thorns remained.

*   *   *

After six months the house was full of flowers. Every vase had been put to use; Alba had taken to drying them, pressing them between old books—anything to preserve their sweetness a little longer. The latest bouquet was propped up in the kitchen sink, still tied up in cellophane and ribbon. It had been sitting there for over a day.

Alba fussed with the flowers, glanced over her shoulder at the policeman sitting at her kitchen table. "Tea? Coffee?" Anything to keep her hands busy.

"No, thanks." The policeman put his hat on the table, running a hand through his short, greying hair. He had a round face: round eyes, round chin, and thick ears that stuck out like satellites.

Alba poured herself a glass of water and sat down across from him. She took a sip to wet her lips, set the glass on the table with trembling hands. "What happens next?"

"We've passed on his details to the Missing Persons Bureau," the policeman said. "We'll try to trace his movements." He paused, looked around the kitchen. "Your husband didn't mention anything about taking a trip?"

She shook her head. "Nothing. We were supposed to go on our *luna de miel*, the honeymoon, a few months ago, but…" A large part of her was relieved, but she couldn't tell the police. What would they think?

They both lapsed into silence. From upstairs came the sounds of movement: the policeman's partner was searching the master bedroom for clues. Yet Alba already knew there was nothing to find. All that remained of Rick were the copious bouquets he had given her and the broken promise they represented.

"Did you and your husband argue recently?" the policeman asked, watching her steadily.

What if he knew the truth? For a moment Alba froze, then she made herself relax. Rick had taught her to be discreet, to be silent. No one could possibly know what had happened between them. Otherwise the neighbours would have intervened a long, long time ago.

"Not more than usual," she said. That, at least, was the truth. She pointed at the flowers in the sink. "He bought me those yesterday."

The policeman looked, admiring the bouquets in the kitchen. "My wife would kill for flowers like these," he said. "Must have cost a small fortune. Your husband must really love you."

"I guess." Alba crossed her arms, touched the bruises hidden by her sleeves and forced a smile. But inside she was hollow. Love? Love was all well and good from afar, but up close it gave more pain than pleasure. No: she was done with love, and it wouldn't contain her any longer.

She glanced around the kitchen, all of a sudden saw the numerous bouquets through the policeman's eyes. The ostentatious display embarrassed her. "You can have them," she said, standing up. She picked up the bouquet in the sink, offered it to the policeman. "Here, for your wife."

"Oh no." He shook his head. "I couldn't."

"Please," Alba insisted. She wasn't strong enough to throw them away yet she wanted them gone. But the policeman just shook his head again and got to his feet as his partner came into the kitchen.

Still clutching the bouquet, Alba walked the policemen to the front porch, even dared to shake their hands when she knew Rick would never have approved.

"Do you have family you could stay with?" the policeman asked.

"I'm okay here." She glanced at the dark space beneath the porch, fought down a shiver. "I'm okay now."

When the police car disappeared around the corner, Alba crouched down and stuffed the bouquet under the porch, until the flowers were swallowed from sight.

*   *   *

The roses were multiplying. Everywhere she turned there were more blooms, more vines, more sharp thorns scratching against the wood-panelled floors. They grew when she wasn't looking, choking the newly installed telephone line, clawing at her arms when she tried to cut them down. And now this: a newly bloomed rose hanging above the master bedroom door as if it had always been there. Alba hugged herself and wondered when she had started going crazy.

Six weeks had passed without a single lead; Rick's name was becoming a permanent fixture on the missing persons' list. Rather than feel relieved, Alba could not help but feel that his spirit still lingered in the house like a smell she could not quite erase.

She ignored the rose hanging above the bedroom door and made her way over to the desk by the window, which looked out onto the next-door neighbour's garden. On the desk was a box of matches and a plate of vanilla-scented candles. Alba took a match, lit each candle one by one. Her every attempt to decorate the house and make her mark on its cold, empty walls had failed, but she refused to relinquish this small act of defiance. Rick had always hated vanilla.

When she was done, she glanced at the rose hanging over the doorway. Did it look slightly bigger than before? Alba ignored the trickle of unease and began to dress for bed. It was only a plant: there was nothing to be afraid of. First thing tomorrow, she would cut it down.

"*Eres muerto*," she told the rose, pulling the covers up to her chin. You're dead.

The rose did not reply.

Alba smiled at her own foolishness, turned over onto her side and let her eyes drift closed. The warm, honeyed scent of vanilla soon lulled her to the edge of sleep, but just as Alba was giving in to the weight and the weariness, she began to notice a faint rustling coming from the door, like skin whispering against skin.

The jolt of fear forced her tired eyes to open. Alba sat upright to shake off the clutches of sleep, listening with growing alarm. Something was slithering towards her open bedroom door, scraping its nails against the walls. It was coming closer, the wooden floorboards in the hallway creaking in warning. A cold sweat gathered at the back of Alba's neck.

"Who's there?" she called. For a moment she wished Rick was there to protect her, to rescue her as he once had. But Rick was never coming back. "Who's there?" she called again, eyes locked on the doorway.

The rustling grew louder. The flickering candles on the desk cast long shadows on the walls that closed in on Alba from every side. She stared at the doorway with her heart in her mouth, clutching a pillow as if it could somehow protect her.

Then there was a dark shadow at head-height in the doorway and Alba realised who it was.

"Rick?" she whispered. "Rick?" Her voice broke.

The shadow did not reply.

Hardly daring to breathe, Alba leaned to the left, stretched out her fingers and flicked on the light switch by her bedside table. The sudden light blinded her: she shadowed her eyes with one hand and dared to hope that her nightmare had disappeared. But when she lowered her hand, the shadow was still waiting, except for it wasn't a shadow nor even the missing Rick.

Swaying in the doorway was a crimson rose as big as Alba's hand, with thick, thorn-tipped vines that coiled down to the ground and stretched further down the hallway, out of sight. The vines shifted, contracted, and all of a sudden the rose was slithering into Alba's bedroom, petals fully extended as if it were taking in every detail.

Alba crossed herself, then pinched her arm, but no: she was awake. The rose snaked further into the bedroom, aiming for the desk on the far wall. It stopped right in front of the candles, its sharply-toothed leaves shuddering angrily. Then, in one smooth swipe, the rose knocked over the plate of candles and sent a spray of hot wax across the desk.

The rose jerked back, then slowly inched forward, examining the still-smoking candles. It circled them once, twice, and still from the hallway came more of its body, slithering into the room. Alba crossed herself again. There was no time to waste: with every second that passed, the patches of clear floor grew smaller. She'd have to tiptoe to the doorway, then make a dash for it.

Ahora, she thought. Alba slipped off the edge of the bed and carefully placed her feet between the vines, first the right foot, then the left. But the rose was ready for her, the bloom swinging around to pin her with its Cyclopean stare. When she began to run, a section of vine whipped around her hand and held her firm, the thorns digging into her flesh.

She screamed, tried to pull away but the thorns dug deeper into her hand and the rose's leaves rattled in warning.

"I'm sorry!" she gasped.

Still the rose squeezed tighter, breaking the skin of her palm and drawing blood.

"I won't escape, I promise! I won't!"

The rose dragged Alba back to the bed, giving her hand a final warning squeeze that brought tears to her eyes. She sank down onto the covers and knew she was defeated.

*   *   *

It was near dawn, the ceiling pinked with the growing light and the room enveloped in stillness. Alba wondered why she was awake; she slept so much these days, her limbs sluggish and unresponsive. Even getting out of bed was a nigh-insurmountable task, and if it weren't for the rose's constant monitoring Alba would have wasted away weeks ago. Instead she was leading a half-life in this bedroom, captive in her own home. She looked down at her wedding ring. This was not what she'd signed up for.

An odd sound from the bedroom window stirred Alba out of her thoughts. She sat up slowly. The rose was curled in loops across on the floor, petals furled up tightly, asleep. Even then she could not tear her eyes away, breathing through her mouth so as not to disturb it.

That sound again. Alba looked, saw a face on the other side of the window. A face! Having been denied companionship for so long, a great yearning stirred within her, but also a great fear. Still the rose slept on, unmoving.

The man in the window—for it was a man, his youthful face outlined with stubble, plaid shirtsleeves rolled up to his elbows—beckoned. Alba glanced at the rose, saw the oval leaves twitch. When the man beckoned again she shook her head. The rose would punish them both if it woke and found him here. It was too dangerous. *Go*, she mouthed, pasting on a smile to let him know she was okay. Her cheeks ached, the expression foreign.

The man shook his head, beckoned more urgently. When she did not react, he felt around the window frame as if to come into the bedroom himself. Alba gasped, held up a hand to stop him, glancing down at the floor. The rose hadn't budged. She closed her eyes in prayer, then released a slow, shaky breath. When she nodded, the man's answering smile made her heart clench.

Alba slid out from under the covers, peered over the edge of the bed to get a lay of the land. The floor was all but covered with vines; she would have to tread carefully. Alba held her breath, placed one foot on the floor, then jerked it back as the rose shifted in its sleep.

She looked at the window and the man nodded encouragingly. There was no getting rid of him unless she told him to leave. She would have to make him understand. Alba gathered her courage. One foot down, then two. She mouthed a quick prayer, then pushed off of the bed. Softly, softly, she tiptoed her way to the desk chair. From there it wasn't far to the window. She climbed onto the desk, winced as it knocked against the wall. Still safe. Soon she was on her knees by the window, separated from the man by a thin pane of glass.

His face was familiar, Alba realised. It was the neighbour, the one she'd taught salsa steps to so long ago. She could not remember his name. Next to him was an older man who barely glanced at her, eyes fixed on the swirls and loops of the rose vines with a peculiar hatred and fascination.

Open the window, the young man mouthed, pointing downwards.

Alba steadied herself on the desk, slid the window up. The cool breeze sent shivers down her arms. She glanced over her shoulder, but still the rose did not stir.

"Hurry up," the man whispered.

Alba stared. "Hurry up?" And then she realised: he was rescuing her. She didn't know whether to laugh or cry. "It's too dangerous!"

"Do you want to stay locked in there forever?" he

snapped.

Alba looked behind her, could not hold back a shudder at the sight of the rose coiled in great loops on the floor, circling the double bed possessively. And yet here she was, almost free without it having noticed.

"Okay," she said. Alba let go of the window frame to climb outside, but the window would not stay open.

"I'll hold it," the man whispered. He braced himself against the sill, propping his shoulder under the window. "Come on!"

Alba lifted her right leg, stuck her foot out the window. She teetered precariously, her left foot bumping against a glass of water on the desktop. They all froze. The glass wobbled but did not spill.

There was a soft dry rattle against the wooden floor; the vines were shifting drowsily. Alba clapped a hand over her mouth to stop herself from screaming. The rose was going to be angry.

The old man spoke, then, for the first time. "If you don't come now, we'll all die."

Alba steeled herself, then half-turned to climb out the window. She placed her right foot on the roof, lowered her head to duck through. Then something pulled on her hair. The rose! She screamed, pushed herself out the window and onto the roof, turning around to find several long strands of her hair caught on the splintering wood of the window frame. But it was too late now, the rose had woken, vines rattling as the petals unfolded, rising from the ground like a snake scenting for prey.

It swivelled to face them and Alba forgot how to breathe.

The rose shot straight out the window and through

the old man in a rush of movement too fast to follow. It withdrew just as quickly, coiling up at the window frame for another attack.

"Father!"

But the old man was gone, falling backwards, his mouth in a wide O that mimicked the great hole in his chest. An arc of blood spattered against Alba's cheek, and she shrank back to the very edge of the roof, praying. They were all going to die.

The rose lunged forward again but this time the young man was prepared. He jumped aside and the window slammed shut, slicing through the rose's vine. The rose's head rolled along the tiles, scattering petals in the wind, until it came to a stop at Alba's feet, twitching. She cried out in disgust, kicked without thinking, and the rose tumbled off of the roof and out of sight.

From inside the house came a terrible thrashing. The man picked himself up, his eyes hardening into narrow slits. He marched over to Alba, pulled her to her feet, dragging her to a ladder propped against the roof. Alba followed him down without protest, her legs shaking beneath her.

As soon as she touched the ground, the man took her arm and led her next door. "Hurry up," he said tightly, and the terrible grief in his voice struck Alba more than anything else that had happened. His father was dead. The old man had died because of her. It didn't seem possible. "You're going to end this," he added.

"This?" She stumbled after him, glancing back at her house. There were no signs of movements but she shuddered anyway. "I don't even know what *this* is."

"A hell rose." He held his front door open, ushered

her through. "A dead man's rose."

*   *   *

It was late evening, but for some reason the birds were still singing loudly in the treetops, half-crooning whistles that echoed down the otherwise silent street. Alba stood in front of her house holding a rifle, staring at the porch steps with dry-mouthed apprehension. Curling out from the dark space under the stairs was a large, thick vine that had burrowed its way through the side wall and into the house. It wasn't moving.

Her neighbour—Sam, she'd finally remembered his name—walked closer and crouched down to examine the vine. "My father recognised what it was the moment he saw it," he whispered. He squinted into the darkness, nodded, then looked up. "The rose was only the bloom. You're going to have to kill the root."

"Me?"

"He's your husband, isn't he?"

"I…" Her mouth went dry. "How do you know it is him?"

For a moment he just looked at her, cool and assessing. Then he said, "Who else would be down there?"

She didn't reply. Alba hefted the gun in her hands, unfamiliar with its weight. "What if someone hears?" Sam was her closest neighbour, but there were houses beyond his, scattered along the darkened street.

"It's silenced," he said dismissively. "And no one hears what they don't want to hear." He stood up, backed away from the steps. "Now, call him." When she hesitated, his face darkened. "You owe me."

Alba swallowed heavily. "Rick?" The first attempt

came out so quiet she had to call his name again.

Silence, then a voice groaned from the depths of the house. "Alba," it said. "Alba…"

The vine around the porch steps shuddered, then began to move as if something were pushing it out from under the house. Alba shrieked, dropped the rifle. She ducked down to pick it up and when she looked again there was a hand wrapped around the edge of the porch steps, and then another, and then an arm, and then a head.

Rick dragged himself out from under the house, leaning on the porch to push himself upright, leaving a trail of skin and liquid on the polished wood. His clothes were threadbare and a thick vine was growing out of his heart, coiling down in loops at his feet. And there it was: a small bullet hole right in the middle of his forehead, enough to kill a normal man, but for some reason it hadn't worked on him. She should have known.

"Alba," he said, and the vine growing out of his chest shuddered in response. "Do you still love me?"

"I never loved you," she replied fiercely, wishing it were true. Her arms trembled with remembered pain and for a moment she was helpless again in front of him.

When she hesitated, he took another step forward. "Why, Alba? Why did you kill me?" White maggots swarmed in his nose and mouth, dripping onto the floor with each word.

In response, Alba lifted the rifle and fired. At this range it was impossible to miss: the bullets tore apart the rest of his decaying face and spattered the wall with blood and wet skin. Rick's body twitched once, twice, then collapsed into a heap on the grass.

"I didn't want to," she told the corpse. "But you made me *really* angry."

THE CURE

I told her it was too late, but she didn't listen. She kept running, pulling me half-stumbling behind her, her hand warm and clammy against mine. The wound on my leg throbbed in time to our steps; the venom was crawling up my veins, poisoning everything it touched. The skin of my calf was already hardening, stiffening, stretched taut over now-bulging muscles.

"It's pointless, Marie! Just leave me and run!"

She looked back, her face a distorted grimace of anger. "Never!" Ahead of us was an abandoned shopping mall. She dragged me through the entrance and up the immobile escalator stairs. The walls were stained with old blood and all the shop entrances were barred shut—the Enemy had been here before.

Marie let go of my hand and ran to the nearest shop, where others like us were cowering behind the safety of bars. She shook the gates, willing them to open. Frightened eyes peered back, unwilling to let us in. "Please," she begged. "Please!" But there was no reply.

I stayed near the top of the escalator, afraid to show myself. I felt dirty, sinful. What if they looked at my face and *knew*? What if the scent of that alien flesh on my leg wafted through my jeans and they realised what I was becoming? There was no cure. They'd never let us in.

Marie ran to the next shop, and the next, begging, pleading, the skin on her hands tearing as she clawed at the bars. But there were sounds coming from downstairs, footsteps coming closer. Marie noticed, came back and wrapped her arms around me, burying her face into the crook of my shoulder. I held her against me for a moment. She smelled of blood and sweetness, and her nose left a warm, wet trail across my skin.

The burning of the venom reached my hip. I grimaced, pushed her away. "Go hide! I'll hold them off."

She shook her head, her hair so greasy it barely moved. After days on the run I didn't look any better. "I'm not leaving you," she said. "They can have me. If we both change, at least…" She threaded her fingers through mine. "At least we'll still be together." Her eyes were wide and frightened, her face smudged with dirt, and she was biting her lip hard enough to split the skin. A fierce, desperate hunger rose within me but this was no time to tell her I loved her.

I pulled my hand free, scanned the area for signs of movement. "Maybe I don't want to be together," I said, low and rough.

"You don't mean that." She hugged me again and I could not bring myself to push her away.

The venom had already reached my stomach: my gut twisted and cramped as it tried to adjust. I groaned as the throbbing spread further up my chest. Soon I would not be worth loving. "Kill me," I mumbled against her lank hair. "Promise you'll kill me."

She didn't answer; I hadn't expected her to.

Eventually Marie pulled away. "I'll find another cure, Jack. I promise." She pressed her lips against mine. I could no longer smell her perfume—all that remained was the stench of rotting meat. Her tongue slipped into my mouth and I gagged.

"No!" she cried. Marie bit down on my lip, *hard*. The shock of sensation bloomed across my face. Before I knew what I was doing, I'd pushed her to the ground and backed away. My face was wet and felt odd, unpleasant. No, more than unpleasant. Was this pain? I touched my lip with one hand and my fingers came away stained red.

I took a step back, then another. My hand… The skin was pink now, fleshy. My veins were green with blood. My chest throbbed strangely as my heart began to beat again. My eyes… I blinked as the film of dead skin cleared and I began to see properly for the first time in months.

Marie crawled towards me, her eyes wide and vacant. I could no longer read the expression in them. She opened her mouth to speak but all that came out was a moan, low and longing. There was a wide hole in her cheek where a piece of shrapnel had torn off the skin. The taste of her kiss on my lips made me gag.

"Hey you!" A blond girl in combat gear stood at the bottom of the escalator. She waved. "Get down here, now! We don't have enough juice to deal with a shopping mall full of zombies!"

Marie was still moving towards me, hand outstretched.

I turned and ran.

SEVEN BIRDS

I. Pears

Beneath the tangy skin is honeyed flesh that dissolves like sweet snow in her mouth. She leans against the tree trunk and bites into the pear again, curves her palm to catch the sticky juices running down her chin. The afternoon sun trickles in through the overhead branches, painting patches of warmth on her arms.

It is 21— and the last Queen of England lies on her deathbed. The Kingdom is about to fall but for now the woman sits in her slice of Eden, her corner of Regent's Park, and eats pears and wonders whether any of the passing men are the right one.

II. Turtle Doves

They meet on a stairway. He notices her first, admires the impractical silver high heels that click-click deliciously against the marble floor. Every step is a challenge. Catch me, those shoes are saying. Catch me if you can.

When she sees him looking, her red lips curve up into a smile and she keeps walking up the stairs in front of him, daring, tempting. Her long, silky hair brushes against her shoulders with every movement, and in that moment he would let her do anything, everything.

She stops on the first floor landing and he follows her through the double doors into the main hall of the museum. She ignores him, stares up at the arched ceilings and the gold-edged frescoes as if they hold the answer to some forgotten question.

"They're beautiful," he says, looking upwards, although he finds art boring and is only here to satisfy the whimsy of a friend.

She looks at him, smiles, looks away. He must do something more to capture her attention.

"I love the birds," he says, then hates himself for sounding so idiotic.

"They look sad," she replies, surprising him. "Their wings were clipped before they learned to fly."

He tells her his name, and civility ensures she returns the favour. The man smiles, sensing victory is close. He takes her unadorned hand with gentle fingers and leaves a warm kiss on her skin that sends shivers down her spine.

The paintings don't seem so interesting anymore, crumbling like the plaster they are made of in the face of his maleness.

III. Hens

The woman's feet are eager, tapping impatiently as she stares into the mirror and applies one last lick of mascara. She smoothes down her clothes, nods at her reflection. As she reaches for her handbag, the doorbell rings.

She flies down the hallway and opens the door to

find him waiting on the other side. Her heart flutters nervously as she drinks in the stubble on his jaw, the form-fitting clothes and steady blue eyes. There is a mischievous curl to his lips when he smiles that almost tempts her to drag him inside. Almost.

"Are you ready?" he asks. She is ready for anything.

As they walk to the tube, he rests his hand on the small of her back and tells her what he has planned for the evening. She barely listens, mesmerised by the warmth of his fingers against her spine. It is the start of something, she is sure of it.

Hours later, they return to her front door. Her cheeks are flushed, whether from wine or excitement she isn't sure. This time when he smiles, she doesn't resist. She turns, opens the door, pulls him inside.

Three steps in and he pins her against the wall. The concrete is cold against her cheek and neck, cold even through the thin layer of her t-shirt. He curls one hand around the back of her neck, lets the other trail down her arm.

He leans in close, and his warm breath against her neck makes her stomach clench. His is the stereotypical aftershave of a fertile male, sweet but invasive, nerve-tingling. She shivers, and he takes that as a cue.

He moves closer, slides his knee between hers. Every inch of their bodies is touching. He runs a hand up her sides, across her stomach…

Then she closes her eyes and is lost in the darkness.

IV. Blackbirds

All the man sees through the coffee shop window is a flash of red lips, but he knows it's her. He throws down his newspaper, hurries out the door, feels the familiar tightening when he glimpses her long, bare calves. Four quick strides and he's by her side.

"Who was she?" the woman says, glancing at the coffee shop. Her shoulders are stiff between his hands and her mouth is a thin line of disapproval.

He glances back, realises what she saw. "Only a friend." When the woman doesn't look convinced he repeats it, a little amused, warmed by her jealousy. What strange publicity this is for love, he thinks.

The woman falls silent, no longer angry but uncertain now. She has given herself away when she had wanted to play cool. He takes in her high cheekbones, the curve of her neck and her delicate blackbird earrings, then feels a surge of tenderness.

"Smoke?" he says, holding up an open packet of Lucky Strikes.

A moment of indecision, then she accepts. She mouths the cigarette so expertly he has to look away.

When he glances back, she's smiling wickedly. "Are you going to ask me out again?"

They're back on familiar territory. He lets one corner of his mouth curl upwards. "Is your lunch hour over?"

"Not yet," she says, pulling him towards her by the collar of his shirt. "Not yet."

V. Golden Rings

They are alone together in this small, intimate parlour, as they have been many times before. It is a room lit only by candles, all soft spaces and round corners. On one side is a small table for two, with a clutter of dirty plates and forks. A half-eaten pear lies forgotten in an empty bowl.

The woman clings to her man tightly as they sway back and forth to the faint strains of music coming from next door. They're a well-matched couple; he in his sharp dark clothes, her in a flowing dress that ends at her knees.

Her hair is pinned up, demure and womanly. Every now and then she looks at the bare patch of skin on her left ring finger and smiles, wondering. He is the right one and if he asks her, she will stay with him forever.

"What are you thinking about?" he asks.

She looks into his eyes and finds a home. She cannot help it when the words slip out.

He hesitates, caught off guard. Love is something they have never discussed but she is patient; she can wait. Rather than force him to reply, she pulls him down for a lingering kiss. Their lips make their re-acquaintance while his fingers dance through her hair, pulling it loose.

The ringing of a telephone interrupts them. He disengages apologetically, answers, then rushes over to turn on the TV.

She follows him, shoves finger-mussed hair out of her face. "What's happened?"

"The Queen is dead," he tells her. To him it seems to herald the end of everything, but she doesn't understand.

VI. Swan's Act

The swans are dying, and they are singing. Beautiful songs, with notes that ripple across the water, leaving London silent in their wake. The sky is grey and cloudless, the wind caresses the docked boats with damp fingertips.

On the bank of the Thames is a young couple in their mid-twenties, him a blond, rugged, Yorkshire lad, her dark-featured and city-slick, delicate beside him. She's cold, he isn't, and they huddle together listening to the swansong.

The next eight minutes change everything.

The woman's heels click-clack on the cobblestones as she walks towards the edge of the water, lured forward by the singing, leaning against her man for support. All that separates the couple from the river is a waist-high metal fence and a steep drop. They could easily jump over that fence but they won't: the water is contaminated.

Paddling on the surface of that water are seven contaminated creatures, seven swans somewhere between alive and dead. Their feathers are more gray than white and their orange beaks are streaked with blood. The stench drifting up from the river is enough to turn the woman's stomach yet she steps closer to the railing, rests her elbows against it to better watch the swans. Such glorious singing.

The man stands beside her and examines the swans carefully. "So it's true," he says. This is his first time near the river since the Queen's death.

"They're beautiful," she replies, but he is not impressed. All he can see are the dull feathers and jagged teeth, all he can hear is a strange crooning. When one of the swans flaps its wings, he notices the rotting tendons and realises it cannot fly.

The woman's eyes are shining. Two of the swans swim in circles around each other and her ribcage all of a sudden feels too small for her heart. She leans against the man, laces her fingers lovingly through his. "They mate for life," she tells him.

He nods, uninterested. He's more concerned by the scientific conundrum before him. Not alive, not dead. It should be impossible.

Across the river are the domed spires of the Tower of London, an ephemeral outline in the mist. It seems somehow wrong that the Tower should endure when everything else has fallen.

"I wonder whether he's still there," the woman says. "The Ravenmaster, tottering out every day to feed the swans as he once fed the ravens." She's smiling as she imagines it; she finds romance in the smallest of things.

He frowns, shakes his head. "He's dead. Fell in. They fished his cane out of the river in Greenwich. The swans left nothing else."

Below them, the swans circle hungrily, singing, ever singing. The tug of the siren-song makes the woman lean further forward, arms and shoulders over the railing. Her cheeks are flushed as she eyes the drop and wonders what it would be like to jump.

The man tightens his grip on her hand. "Don't."

But she is mesmerised by the swans and how they glide around each other, and their singing creates such a pleasurable ache in her heart that she is all of a sudden convinced they're singing about love, about undying love. The realisation makes the swans even more beautiful. "Through sickness and through health," she says softly.

When the woman looks up from the river she finds the man studying her as if she were some scientific conundrum he cannot understand.

She smiles at him. "You wanted to ask me something?" She has had her answer ready for weeks: yes, yes, yes.

The man pauses. "Not here." He wants the swans gone; they make him uncomfortable. How the woman can trick herself into seeing something that is not there is beyond him. She seems so foolish and simple for believing that illusion.

"Here is perfect," she says. "Just say it."

And because the words have been on the tip of his tongue all day, the man acquiesces, turning away from the woman to face the Tower once more. He leans against the railing, looks down at the swans and imagines crushing them under his foot. "It's over," he says. He says it twice as if one hurt wasn't enough. "It's over."

The woman steps back, steps back again, away from the stench of the river and from the swansong which all of a sudden has gone flat to her ears. She looks at the back of the man's head but cannot find an explanation. "Over?"

He turns around with a ready smile and a prepared list of platitudes, but he never gets the chance to use them.

The woman charges forward, shoves him. No time to scream. The man topples over the railing and down into the river below.

FAMILY MATTERS

My brother died on a crisp Thursday morning, when most of Islington was still in bed and the doorsteps were peppered with uncollected rubbish. I didn't hear him go, didn't even notice he'd died until three days later when his finger fell off playing Pro Evo. He ate his finger before I could sew it back on and then went back to his videogames.

"I'm starting to think your brother will never get a 9 to 5 job," Dad told me when he called that evening.

I glanced at Neal. He was staring blankly at the TV, trying to change channels on the remote with his missing index finger. The TV refused to budge from Channel 4 and its ridiculous programme about improbable weddings.

Dad sighed, oblivious. "He'll never change. I'm really coming to the conclusion that he's never going to leave academia."

"Well, he has been at university for seven years now," I said, pulling my blanket tighter around my shoulders as I trudged towards the kitchen. As I passed the bathroom, I breathed through my mouth so as not to smell the blood. "It can't really be that much of a surprise anymore."

"I know, I know." But he didn't, not really. I had to bite my tongue to stop myself from saying anything stupid.

Once in the kitchen, I tucked the phone between my cheek and shoulder, opened the fridge and looked inside. There were two packages of sirloin steak from Sainsbury's on the top shelf, with big round stickers: 2 for £5! I dropped one pack onto the counter, then rooted through the freezer for peas.

"What are you doing?"

"Making dinner. Steak, chips and peas." The thought of warm food cheered me: with the heating off to stop Neal from decaying, I'd discovered that the kitchen was the coldest room in the house. I resisted the urge to turn on the boiler, rubbing my hands together.

"Ah, of course. Your brother has always liked meat."

That was about as true as me still liking fluffy pink kitten birthday cards now that I was twenty-three. I dumped the largest steak, rare and bloody, on a plate, then set the other aside to cook. "He likes meat even more now," I said, half-smiling.

"Then he would love Argentina. There's so much meat there!"

I heard the drag-drag of feet, turned around to find my brother standing at the kitchen doorway, looking as hopeful as a corpse could. He reached out to grab the raw steak and I smacked his hand away, shaking my head firmly. *No snacking*, I mouthed.

"Anna?"

"Sorry, Dad. I got distracted."

"Is your brother there? Can I speak with him?"

"Oh, he's just gone into the bathroom." I smacked my brother's hand away from the steak again, then pointed at the bathroom door when he began to look grumpy. He shuffled away slowly.

"I wanted to speak with him yesterday but he wasn't answering his phone."

"It's not working properly, I think. Maybe the battery has died, or something else has died… We're looking for a solution."

"Ah well," Dad sighed. "I'll speak to him next time then. But things are okay between you?"

"I guess." I checked on the chips in the oven, then began heating oil in a pan for the steak. "We've been living together for a while now, so we've settled into a routine. Sometimes he makes me angry, but family matters more than that in the end." I huddled over the pan, savouring the only source of heat in the house.

"Anyway, it could be worse," I added.

My brother reappeared in the kitchen doorway, chewing on a forearm he had retrieved from the bathroom. Judging by the scraps of material, it was all that was left of the postman.

"It could be a lot worse, actually," I said. "At least now he cleans up after himself."

Belle arrived at the café twenty minutes late, by which time Eddie had successfully devised forty-two different ways to kill the smug werewolf behind the counter. Only thirteen of those ways involved eye witnesses, but the two most satisfying would leave Eddie with permanently disfigured hands.

Jace—the werewolf—remained entirely oblivious to Eddie's unpleasant intentions. He greeted Belle cheerily, in that overly familiar ex-boyfriend way that made Eddie's throat burn with jealousy and hunger. As soon as Belle looked away, Jace's mouth dropped into a sneer and he glared at Eddie. *You're dumped*, he mouthed, drawing a line across his neck. And, because Belle was looking at him, Eddie could do nothing but smile. Luckily, three hundred years of vampirism had gifted him with a very pleasant smile indeed.

"Sorry I'm late," Belle said, not looking sorry at all. If anything, her darting eyes indicated she wouldn't have minded being more late, or even not turn up at all.

Eddie ignored the growing dread, blaming his anxiety on Jace's behaviour. "What's twenty minutes to an immortal?" he joked, helping Belle into her seat. It was a bloody long time, that's what it was, but there was no point complaining to a woman. He settled into the chair opposite her, caught a whiff of wet dog from Jace. "We should have met in our usual place," he said, wrinkling his nose. "It stinks here."

"Oh really?" Belle fidgeted, pulled her cardigan tighter around her shoulders. "I hadn't noticed."

He tapped the tip of his nose, winked. "I'm a little more sensitive."

"But not emotionally, right?" Her laughter was forced, high-pitched, so unlike her usual dry chuckle that all of Eddie's fears were confirmed. He glanced away only to see Jace gloating, then looked down at his hands.

"Belle," he said softly. "Don't do this to me."

She froze. "Don't do what?"

His eyes flashed up to hers, but he said nothing.

"Oh, Eddie." Belle sighed, and the expression on her face turned his gut to stone. "Look," she began, "I really value and respect your opinion, you know that, right? You're really important to me. It's just... I don't think it's working out, and I don't want to lose your friendship. I just... I just want us to be friends."

Friends. She couldn't have been clearer. Eddie kept his face blank. What use did a vampire have for human friends? He had his clan for companionship. It was the other stuff that he wanted, the feel of living skin and the pulse of beating hearts, and the warmth of love in a life of darkness.

"Friends," he said flatly. "Of course."

Belle was too human to notice the tiny inflections in his voice. She smiled, relieved. "I'm so glad we could agree on this. You're really important to me and I was afraid that if I told you I'd met someone el—" She bit her lip. "Oops?"

Eddie closed his eyes briefly, then opened them. "Tell me it's not that Jace boy."

Belle laughed, flicked her hair over her shoulder. "No way! Get real. What made you think of that?"

"He knew you were going to leave me today."

"Oh." Belle bit her lip, looked away briefly. "That's kinda because… Well, I dumped him in this café too." She rested her head on one hand, smiled sheepishly. "This is my break up café."

Eddie frowned, wondering what she saw in the greasy 24-hour café that made it suitable for heartbreak. Maybe it was the stink of fast food and werewolves, which encouraged patrons to leave quickly. Maybe it was nostalgia, or a way of grouping bad memories into one place to keep their taint contained.

"Could you at least tell me why?" Eddie finally said.

Belle chewed her lip, toying with the salt shaker as she thought. "I guess the whole self-denial thing was cute—" she noticed his grimace "—sweet, I mean, romantic really, but it's gotten a bit… boring?" She reached over and squeezed his hand gently.

He withdrew his hand. "Boring? The fact that I can rip your throat out is boring? That I have to fight not to sink my teeth into you and drink your blood? That's boring?"

She sighed, played with her hair. "You know what I mean," she said. "Vampires are so common now, and everyone's dating one. It's just not cool. There's no thrill in it anymore."

"Is that what you're missing? The thrill? Because I can do scarier. You haven't even seen me in scary mode yet. Seriously." He smiled, fierce, hoping the sight of some fang would make her heart flutter like it once did.

But she was unmoved. "We both know you'd never actually do it, and girls want guys that know what they want and take it."

"Like this new guy," he replied sourly, and she nodded.

She reached forward and grabbed his hand again, unaware that her neck was tipped towards him, bare and exposed. The perfect temptation. He wanted to bite but he wouldn't let himself. Eddie grit his teeth and wondered when he'd become so predictable.

"Oh, Ed," she said, leaning towards him. "Please say we can remain friends. I love Tom but you'll always have a place in my heart, you know that, right?"

"Of course, Belle," he said, hating himself. "Whatever you want."

Her answering smile made him sick with happiness. "Please say you'll meet Tom, too, Ed. I've told him so much about you."

Tom. It couldn't be a more human name. Eddie imagined a scrawny teenaged boy with sandy blond hair and the common sense of a weasel. He smiled politely. "What's this Tom like?"

Her face flushed, her eyes sparkled. "He's great! He ticks all the right boxes, he's a bad boy with that slouchy-I-don't-care style. And he's strong and fearless and possessive." She laughed softly. "Even more than you, if that's possible!"

Belle gestured expansively, knocking over the salt shaker. "It's just like in the old days, when I first started dating you. Everyone says I'm crazy, that he's dangerous, that love cannot exist between us… It's all *so* romantic."

Every word felt like a stake to Eddie's heart, but he

couldn't blame her: he'd asked for it. Eddie stood. "I'm glad to hear it. You deserve more than what I can give you. You deserve life and family with a human boy."

Belle stood as well, puzzled. "Oh, Tom's not human."

Eddie was about to ask Belle what type of supernatural could possibly trump a vampire, when the café door swung open and a young man stumbled in, bringing with him the stench of decay. His dark blond hair was streaked with dirt, his mouth open in a soundless snarl.

Eddie stepped back, alarmed, exchanging anxious looks with Jace, but Belle waved cheerfully at the newcomer. "Hi, Tom!"

DATING THE UNDEAD

Reasons Why A Zombie is Better Than A Man

1. A zombie doesn't care what you look like.

Belle twisted in front of the mirror nervously, smoothing down the satin of her black dress. She hated her body, the soft curve of her belly and the way it was impossible to hide her cleavage unless she dressed like a nun. But what she hated most were her legs and the way they stuck out of the bottom of her dress like shapeless sausages.

She went up onto her tiptoes, wondering how slimming a pair of heels could be, then sighed. "What do you think, darling? Do my thighs look big in this?"

Inside his cage, her boyfriend Tom was pressed up against the metal barrier, reaching through the bars with rotting fingertips, just as eager to have her as always.

Belle chewed her lip thoughtfully. "Guess it doesn't make me look fat, then."

2. A zombie doesn't expect you to cook.

There was only one microwave meal left in all of Tesco, a decidedly ungenerous portion of fish pie that would barely satisfy one person. Belle wandered up and down the ready meal section, shaking her head in dismay. What would they have for dinner? She couldn't go looking down the other aisles, with their loose vegetables and packets of flour. She needed food, not ingredients!

The third time she passed by the microwave meal she picked it up, if only to safeguard it from the sticky paws of other shoppers. She turned the package over in her hands, considering, but no: it wasn't enough for them both. She began to put the fish pie back down reluctantly.

"I'll have that," a man in a business suit said, grabbing it from her hands.

Belle spluttered a protest, tried to tell him she'd changed her mind, but the man didn't have the chance to respond. Two rotting hands wrapped around the man's neck, choking him more effectively than the tie around his neck. He gurgled, feet kicking out, flailing as he dropped the microwave meal onto the floor.

Tom's half-decayed face was twisted into a grin as he dragged the man within biting range. He sank his teeth into the man's thick, fleshy neck with undisguised relish.

Belle beamed and bent down to pick up the microwave meal. "Great, that's dinner sorted!"

3. A zombie cleans up after himself.

The doorbell rang.

"Would you get that, honey?"

Tom was already by the front door, pulling on the lever system she'd installed to turn the handle for him. He shuffled back to let the door swing open, then latched onto the milkman before the man could escape

The milkman screamed, tried to run away, but Tom already had the man's wrist in his mouth. He bit down, tore clean through the bone. The milkman's hand thudded onto the front porch but Tom ignored it, intent on bigger prey.

The milkman scrambled backwards, looking at his bleeding stump, his mouth wide open, no sound escaping from his lips except a high-pitched whine. Tom lumbered after him, grabbed hold again, then bit and bit until the man stopped moving.

Belle picked up the milk bottles at the doorstep with the tips of her fingers, holding them as far away from her body as possible. The bottles were flecked with blood, but luckily none of the bone chips had pierced the foil.

She stepped back to return inside, felt something brush against her foot, and looked down to find the milkman's severed hand.

Belle frowned and kicked the hand off of the porch, towards Tom. "Clean that up, would you?"

Tom snatched up the hand and put it into his mouth.

4. A zombie likes you for your brains.

"All these men hit on me all the time, and they only care about sex," Belle said angrily. "They come up to me, tell me I'm the most beautiful girl they've ever seen… Who do they think they're kidding?"

"Graah," said Tom.

"They don't ask me what I think about religion or politics or things like that. They don't care what I think. And I *do* think, a lot! About world peace and… and yeah!"

"Graaaaah."

"Oh, sorry, darling. I'm ranting. Of course you know all of this already. And you're not like them at all: you really listen. Come here and give me a kiss.

"Hey, why are you grabbing my head? Ow! No need to squeeze so hard, darling, ow! Get off! If you bring those teeth of yours near my skull, I'll—!"

5. A zombie doesn't care what's on the telly.

"You're so lucky," Amanda said, curled up on the couch next to Belle. The two were dressed in their pyjamas, swathed in blankets, huddling around a bowl of popcorn. "I never get to watch Emo Vampires at home. My boyfriend *hates* the series."

Belle was suitably scandalised. "But how can he hate it?! There's vampires and emo boys and emo vampires. What's not to like?"

"I know, right? But it's always on at the same time as the football, so he just brings his friends over and claims the TV." Amanda sighed.

"Tom would never do that to me," Belle said, smug. She raised the volume to cover up the neighbour's screams. "He doesn't care what's on the telly."

6. A zombie can protect you.

Belle groaned, pulling her pillow over her face. The student house three doors down was having an impromptu Sunday evening house party, and the thumping music had been boring a hole into her skull for hours.

She glanced at the digital clock on her bedside table. 3:00 AM.

"That's it," Belle muttered, gathering her courage.

She picked up the home phone and dialled, wincing when a drunken voice bellowed a hello.

"Hi there. This is your neighbour, in number 17. Some of us need to work tomorrow morning, so if you could turn the music down, that would be great."

"What?" the voice yelled back. "Can't hear you!"

"It's Belle, from house 17—"

"No way! A booty call, rock on! I'll be over in five."

"No, I—" The line went dead.

Nine minutes later, drunken voices filled her front yard. Belle peered out of her bedroom window, only to be met by catcalls. Seven boys stood on her lawn, cheering and yelling, beer bottles in hand. One of them downed the contents of his bottle and smashed it against the wall of her house.

She pulled up her window. "Go away!"

The boys just shouted back. Belle realised with growing horror that a couple of them were trying to find a way into the house, testing the ground floor windows, trying the door, calling out lewd suggestions.

They kicked open the front door, ran inside, and that's when the screaming started. Tom made sure that not a single one reached her bedroom.

7. A zombie never talks back.

"I can't *believe* you tried to follow some other girl home! What were you thinking?"

Tom just stood there, not even trying to move.

"What am I saying? You clearly weren't thinking. You've the intelligence of an underdeveloped pig," she snapped. She slammed her grocery bags on the kitchen counter, began to unpack with stiff, jerky movements.

Not even the two kilos of lean ground mince got Tom's attention, but after the number of students he had eaten the day before, Belle was not surprised.

"You're not to leave the house without me," she continued. "I don't care what you say."

Still no response.

"And from now on, you need to eat outside. No bloody tracks in this house anymore!"

No reaction. She looked at Tom's face to see if he was ignoring her, but no, he simply had nothing to say. One side of his mouth was sagging listlessly, as if out of deep guilt.

"So you'll do everything I say?"

When Tom kept standing there quietly, Belle smiled, appeased. "That's decided, then."

8. A zombie is environmentally aware.

"The road's so much quieter than I remember," Belle's mother said, looking around the house while she sipped from her cup of Lady Grey. "And the neighbours, too."

"That's Tom's doing entirely," Belle gushed. "He's done so much to reduce noise pollution in the area."

"I still think there's something funny about him," Belle's father said. "I don't care what you say. You're my daughter; I've got a right to be protective."

"The garden's looking splendid, too," her mother continued, casting Belle a sympathetic glance. "What fertiliser do you use? Perhaps we should buy some too."

"Oh, I wouldn't know exactly. Tom got it for me from some of the university students. He's very environmentally aware, you know. Why, he refuses to use a car and walks everywhere!"

Her father was not impressed. "He's probably one of those idiots who eats that weird hippy shit."

"Only organic food, actually," Belle replied primly.

9. A zombie's mother will never drop by.

A thump against the front door.

Belle sighed, rinsed off the plate she was washing, then stacked it to dry and peeled off her gloves. She'd trained Tom to open the door weeks ago—what on earth was he doing knocking?

Another thump.

"Coming, honey!" Belle hurried to the front door, opened it only to find an overweight woman in shapeless beige three-quarter length trousers and a black tank top. The woman's face was decayed beyond recognition, her long teeth gleaming through the rotted gaps in her cheeks.

The woman took a step forward, reaching out with long, desperate fingers.

Belle looked over the woman's shoulder. Tom was happily distracted by the remains of a postman.

"Tom!" she called. He didn't look up. "Is this your mother, Tom?"

She took his lack of reply as a no, reached for the shotgun beside the door, and blasted the woman's brains into tiny pieces.

10. There's no competition for the shower in the morning.

A cold draft of air entered the bathroom, stealing all the warmth from her shower. Belle scowled, poked her head around the shower curtain. Her boyfriend was standing in the doorway, looking right at her.

"I got here first," she told him crossly. "So get out and let me finish getting ready."

Tom ignored her and took a slow step into the bathroom. So that was how it was going to be.

Belle scowled. "I got here first, and the sooner you get out, the sooner I'll finish."

"Graaaaah!" He tripped on a bath mat, slammed onto the ground. As he pushed himself up, his nails tore shreds out of the mat. Then he looked right at her with all the good humour of someone who hasn't eaten in days.

Belle jumped out of the shower, soap suds still trailing down her spine. "Okay, okay, we're not competing, that's fine, you go ahead first."

But instead of walking past, Tom dashed her head against the sink and delicately scooped out her brains. When he was finished eating, he stepped over the corpse, into the shower, and began to rinse off the blood.

THE PERFECT SONG

Want a brew?

Those were the three words that had led to everything, that had led to this, him semi-conscious on his living room couch surrounded by scraps of torn paper and broken pens. But he had done it, and that's what mattered most. He had written the world's most perfect song. If he'd had the energy, Michael would have smiled.

A high-pitched ringing roused him from his stupor. He unpeeled his face from the leather armrest and sat up slowly, wiping his nose on his sleeve. His hand trembled; the tips of his fingers had begun to turn brown. Everything in the room was painfully sharp, from the hard edges of the flat screen TV to the spiky row of books along the wall.

His phone was still ringing. He shoved a hand down the side of the couch, retrieved the offending object and brought it up to his face to glare at the screen. It was his drummer, Dave, a short, weedy guy whose only saving grace was a sense of rhythm that put tap dancers to shame. Michael placed the phone on his lap, crossed his arms and studiously ignored it. *He* called the shots. *He* was the one with the genius, the feverish touch of inspiration. That their band had rocketed up the charts was Michael's doing alone.

Two self-indulgent sighs later, the phone stopped ringing. Then it buzzed angrily, the screen flashing: one new message. If curtness was a measure of anger, Dave was beyond pissed.

Band practice. Tonight. Six. Be there.

Michael deleted the message without replying. He'd be there, alright. He'd show Dave, feed his fame-hungry mouth with yet another chart-topper. He tossed his phone onto the couch, then leaned forward to grab the small pot on the coffee table, his stomach cramping with the movement. The feel of cold metal against his skin was uncomfortable but he ignored the sensation and brought the pot closer to his face, peering inside. It was empty. There was no tea left, just four defeated teabags, crumpled together at the bottom. He needed to make more.

But first, first he'd reread the lyrics.

Michael put down the pot and began rooting through the crumpled pages on the tabletop, slowly at first, then with growing urgency. It was here somewhere; he remembered writing the words, wrestling the rhymes into place. But all he could find was papers covered in swirling patterns, in scribbles, in child's drawings: sharks eating fish, question marks, light bulbs, and spirals, endless spirals.

He hadn't drawn these! Where was his song? Where was everything he'd been working on for the last two weeks? His heart was pounding in his chest, every beat another nail in his coffin. The panic thickened in his throat. Swallowing didn't push down the fear.

Michael grabbed another page, knocked the pot off of the table and froze as it crash, crash, crashed on the wooden floor. A trickle of brown liquid seeped from the spout as it lay there, inert, the echo of its fall still ringing in Michael's ears. After a few long moments he straightened, took three deep breaths to calm down. It was fine. He could write the song again. The words were in his head; he didn't need the paper.

There were chewed up pens on the ground. Michael took one, then selected one of the cleaner pieces of paper. He flattened the page against the tabletop, trying to iron out the creases. It took a certain concentration to get the pen to sit right in his hand; it kept slipping, trying to escape. Finally, he managed to place the tip of the pen against the whiteness. Thus posed, Michael waited for the familiar surge of inspiration.

Nothing happened. The antique clock on the mantelpiece—his grandfather's—ticked loudly, reminding him of the deadline: six hours until band practice. With every passing moment the ticking grew louder, pounding alongside his heart. His bones ached at the sound, and he couldn't focus, not like this. So he reached under the table and grabbed the remote. The TV blared into existence, loud at first, then quieter, quieter, as he turned the volume down. The sound of voices was comforting.

Now he could write. Michael forced himself to start, scrawling out a jagged 'the'. It didn't look right. He drew a line through it, tried writing 'and'. That was wrong, too. He crossed it out, glared at his traitorous hand. Pen against the paper again, waiting for inspiration, but the words didn't come. The words didn't come.

Nothing. He had nothing. He *was* nothing. Not a musician, not a man, not a breath of air. Not even a speck of dust, nor a word nor a letter nor a question mark. All he was, was…

Yes, that was it. Wasted space. Emptiness.

There was a constant pressure on him, forcing him to write, to create, but ever since his fiancée funeral, when he'd stood to say a few words and *felt* his speech shrivel up in his mouth, the words hadn't come anymore. Not by themselves. He needed tea, and he needed it now. A cup of tea solved everything.

Michael pushed himself off the couch, wrapping the blanket around him to offset the cold. The walk to the kitchen was painful, his legs trembling beneath him, and he was driven forward only by the growing need for a shot of warmth.

Want a brew?

Those were the three words that had started everything, that had led to this, to him rooting through the kitchen, leaving a wake of opened cupboards and drawers behind him as he desperately tried to remember where he'd hidden his stash.

There! On the top shelf! Michael put a knee on the counter, reached upwards with trembling hands. In his anxiety the box slipped from his fingers and tipped over, contents tumbling onto the linoleum floor.

No! He pushed himself off of the counter, scrambled around on his hands and knees, shoving teabags into the front pocket of his hoodie. There were only five. He looked under the counters, but no, that was all. Five. He had to buy more, and soon.

But first, a cup of tea. He needed it *now*, his mouth was going dry, he could feel the shakes setting in. Just one cup, and he'd write the damn song again and go to band practice, get the day over and done with. Then he could come back home and drink more tea to forget that anyone outside the door existed. The only person that mattered was gone.

Michael took a teabag out of his pocket and held it in a tight fist as he stumbled towards the kettle, a cylinder of silvery-metal that distorted his reflection and turned him into a smudge of a man, an abstract drawing. His face was scrawny, leathery, the deadened brown skin on his face a mark of his growing habit. He touched his cheek, winced at the smell of rot on his fingertips.

One more song, he thought. The perfect song, a tribute to his fiancée and their love, to what should have been their future. He'd wear deodorant and concealer to band practice tonight and then… and then… He'd clean up his act as soon as he was done recording, Michael decided, nodding slowly at first, then more decisively. Valerie would have liked that.

He popped open the kettle, peered inside. There was no water, only a thick layer of calcium coating the sides. Michael grabbed the kettle and brought it with him the two steps it took to get to the sink, then paused, flummoxed. The sink was full of dirty old dishes—mugs, mostly—and there was a saucer of congealed burger, dark brown with age. A part of Michael wanted to take that meat and eat it, raw and rotted as it was. But the longing for tea was stronger.

He put down the kettle, took a dirty mug and looked at the old tea rings staining the bottom and sides. A shrug, then Michael tossed the teabag inside and picked up the kettle once more to fill it. But there were too many dishes stacked in the sink and they wouldn't budge no matter how hard he tried to wrestle the kettle under the tap. And there was so little time; his shaking was getting worse, he felt weak, worthless.

It didn't matter, it didn't matter. Forget the water. He couldn't wait. Michael threw the kettle onto the counter, reached for the mug. The teabag was stuck to the bottom; he had to squeeze his fingers in and scrape at it with his nails to get it out. There was a strange sound, a ripping and pulling on his index finger. Michael examined his hand, noticed with distant interest that the yellowed, cracked nail of his index finger was hanging loose. He pulled it off and reached into the mug again.

There! He took out the teabag, tried to rip it open, but his clumsy hands were slow to respond. He resorted to his teeth, gnawing at the corner, pulling, tearing. When the hole was big enough, he tilted his head back and tipped the contents into his mouth. The bitterness of the leaves wracked a shudder through his spine but he kept chewing, forced his mouth to create enough saliva to trigger the high. As the rush kicked in his chewing slowed and the angles of the room grew rounded in their softness.

Relieved, Michael trudged out of the kitchen, taking the mug with him. He paused in the hallway to place a dry kiss on the framed photo of Valerie. Her smile shone brightly even in the darkness of the hall and he was momentarily tempted to take her to the living room to see her face by daylight, but then he remembered his fingertips, his leathery skin, and his hand fell away from the frame. He couldn't let her see him like this. After, when it was all done, he'd bring her picture out, but not yet. Not like this.

Michael returned to the living room, his limbs heavy and pleasurably numb. He sank down onto the couch, pulled the soft cotton blanket more firmly around his shoulders, and picked up his pen again. This time it fit into his hand like a missing limb, a perfect match. He was ready. And this time he was going to write something different, something better. A truly perfect song.

He placed the tip of the pen against the paper and wrote the first word. Was it too obvious? Michael looked up, thinking, and the glare of the TV caught his eye. In the scrolling headlines at the bottom of the screen was a word that caught his attention: 'tea'. It couldn't be a coincidence.

Four hurried taps on the remote's volume button, and he could hear the voices clearly.

"—was never meant for public consumption." The speaker was a balding, portly Indian man, wearing a white lab coat and circular round glasses that barely covered his eyes. "Tea has undisputed *medicinal* properties, but to allow unregulated consumption is sheer folly. Unchecked, an addict's nervous system will mutate extensively, as is already happening in London, leading to increased aggression and—" he paused, awkward "—and appetite."

Mutants in London, Michael thought, amused. He jotted down the doctor's words on one side of the page. Maybe he could work that into the chorus. Valerie had always wanted to visit London.

The view switched back to the main studio, to that woman with the ever-perfect blonde bob, eternal smile, and sharply geometric suit. "Thank you, Dr Parkeesh." She turned to face the camera directly. "Dr Parkeesh is one of the court experts in the ongoing trial against John Tetley, who began selling tea in England two months ago as a herbal alternative to anti-depressants."

Tetley, Michael wrote, in a looping scrawl. The pleasurable buzz was fading, leaving behind a heaviness that made him sleepy, the warmth of the tea settling into his bones. He traced the word again with his fingertip. The curve of the 'y' tapered off into a small spiral that reminded him of Roy, his dealer.

The phone was in his hand before he knew what he was doing. He dialled Roy's number, breathing slowly as he waited for Roy to pick up. The clock on the mantelpiece was ticking leisurely, unhurried, and Michael relaxed. There was loads of time before band practice.

"Hello? Mike?"

"Roy. Hey." Michael paused, then realised what it was he wanted. "I need some more brew." As he spoke, he began doodling on the page, drawing a little mug in one margin.

"God, Mike, what're you doing with that stuff? I sold you a box last week!"

When Michael replied, his voice had a sharp edge that he didn't recognise. "Are you going to give me more, or do I need to find someone else?"

"You're not gonna find anyone else. Supply's dried up. Borders are closed. Thank God." Roy was nervous. "Look, man. Don't take any more of that shit. Haven't you been watching the news?"

No. No, no, no. Roy was lying. "I'll buy everything you've got left in cash, up front." He still had two guitars; he could sell those. Didn't Roy understand that he needed tea to write? He was nothing without his writing. He was no one. "Please, Roy, I need it."

There was a long silence. For a moment Michael was afraid the line had died, then Roy spoke, slowly and carefully. "You haven't got any of those symptoms yet, right? 'Cause you know I'd be forced to report you."

"Symptoms?"

"Darker skin, infection, you know, that kinda stuff. The stuff they talked about on that emergency broadcast last night." Roy's voice sharpened. "You saw that, right?"

"Yeah, yeah." Michael looked at his index finger, at the tender skin where the nail had ripped off. "I'm fine, relax. I just need one more dose, okay? One more, then I'm clean." He fought to keep his voice even, could feel the desperate anger bubbling under his skin.

"You're not listening, man," Roy said. "I've got nothing. Delivery never made it. Britain's in lockdown, for Chrissake." He sighed. "Trust me, you're better off."

Michael threw his phone across the room. It smacked into the wall with a loud crunch that did nothing to satisfy his anger. He should've known Roy wouldn't understand. Roy didn't have to deal with friends and family and strangers begging for new songs, thinking that the words came easy when he had to struggle with every single one. Roy was jealous of his fame, of the vapid girls throwing themselves at him when all he wanted was to see Valerie again. Roy had to be lying.

Tetley. Michael looked up instinctively when he heard the word. He'd forgotten the TV was on.

The news anchor's eternal smile looked more like a grimace. "John Tetley, along with his co-conspirator Paul Tips, are suspected of being involved in the contamination of London's water resources, leading to a mass addiction of tea that has resulted in riots. Travel in the area is now highly restricted, and the Royal

Courts of Justice have issued an injunction against all tea manufactures. Benjamin Clerk is on the scene. Ben?"

Ben was a skinny man in his mid-twenties, with tousled sandy-blond hair. His black square-framed glasses meant business, as did the set frown on his face, but despite it all he looked like a school boy, desperate to please. He was standing in a wide square, one of London's landmarks, and was dwarfed by a giant black statue of a lion that frowned at Michael through the TV, its dark eyes heavy and brooding.

The lion stared right at Michael as if it knew that he was a failure. Michael tried to ignore it, to focus instead on what Ben was saying, but the lion's eyes burned into his cracked lips. He wiped away the loose tea leaves, tried to chew less obviously, yet the lion still stared, still judged. Michael looked away, picked up the pen—when had he dropped it?—and tried to write a couple words, but all that came out was a question mark.

More tea, that would fix it. He grabbed the mug, spat the chewed-up leaves out, then took a fresh teabag out of his hoodie and ripped it open, shakily pouring the contents into his mouth. The rush wasn't as strong this time but it took the edge off of things. When he looked back at the TV, the lion was smiling.

That's why he'd started drinking tea in the first place. He'd tried all the usual stuff—alcohol, painkillers—anything that would make reality a little less real, erase the image of that open casket, the auburn hair and long lashes pressed tightly together. Nothing had worked, but then, two months ago on a tour of Europe, it had just been there, on offer, so tempting, and someone had said those three words. The overweight man in the faded band t-shirt had pulled him aside and said those words:

Want a brew?

He'd only smoked the leaves at first, but it did nothing, a little high, a tingle of warmth down his spine. Then he'd tried it properly, sweetened with sugar and milk to take the edge off of the bitterness, and… God. The high was worth it, even though he hated hot drinks, hated warm liquid against his teeth and tongue.

It soon grew easier to have hot drinks, to drink tea until that was all he could do and he couldn't imagine *not* drinking it, and he was sneaking off into the bathroom during gigs for a quick fix to carry him through the night. Until he was back here, home alone with nothing left but the yellow teeth of an addict, a lost cause. Not even the words would come. What would Valerie have said? His music, all that defined him, was gone, and in its place was an empty, lonely hunger that would never be satisfied.

The thought was too painful; he had to have more tea to numb the burning of his emotions. Michael fished the three remaining teabags out of his pocket and lined them up in a row on his knee. He patted down his hoodie to make sure it was empty and that's when he heard it: a rustle of paper. He reached into his pocket again and his fingers brushed against smooth, hard edges. Slowly, just barely, hope began to beat in his chest once more.

He pulled it out of his pocket. It was a piece of paper, folded six times. The song. The perfect song. He unfolded it with trembling fingers. The paper was stiff, reluctant to give up its secrets. But he was patient. There was time.

When there was only one fold left, Michael placed the paper on the tabletop. On that page were the words that would save him, the song that would buy him back all the respect he'd lost. He thought of Valerie's proud smile in the hallway, of how she'd look hung up on the living room wall.

Michael slid his fingers between the two layers, took a deep breath, then unfolded the page flat against the tabletop.

His heart stopped. One word stared up at him, repeated over and over across the page in his own loopy handwriting. This was his perfect song. This was the best he could write.

Without looking away from the page, Michael reached for the three teabags on his knee and placed them into his mouth one by one. He worked his tongue around them slowly, sucking on them, seeing the jagged edges of the word in front of him begin to blur.

He grew sleepier, and sleepier still, his eyelids heavy as he lent his head on the tabletop, forehead pressed against the page. This close he could barely read it but it didn't matter anymore. Nothing mattered anymore.

Want a brew?

Those were the three words that had led to nothing, that had led to this. The thing that was once Michael lumbered to its feet and headed outside, hunting for someone to fill up the emptiness.

ALIVE

The drink is going to my head so I bump my hip against his because now I can, I have an excuse. He looks at me through the corner of his eye and I admire the sharp line of his jaw, the way his lips purse over that hand-rolled cigarette. Here, in the corner of the pub, drinks in our hands, the play of our bodies goes unnoticed by our colleagues.

When the others go home we dance in the darkest corner, his arms around me and mine around him. My heart keeps time with the hot breath on my neck. Each beat is a victory. Alive. Alive. Alive.

When I wake up alone the next morning the excitement has already faded. The laughing girl of yesterday is someone I do not recognise. I trudge into work and even his face is different—deader. But we are all dead, here. Our lives are going nowhere and it is only the brief moments of pleasure that make us forget.

I sit at my desk and eight hours blur by; soon I am home and staring at the street outside. It is cold by the window. I wrap a blanket around my shoulders and watch people shuffle past, heads down to the ground, seeing no one, touching nothing.

He tries to catch my eye again at work but I ignore him. It's not safe. He makes my chest ache and my mind turn in pointless circles. Then I hate myself for cowering in the safety of inaction. I take up smoking. It's a punishment and a blessing, one pain to subdue another.

The sickness comes as a relief. I shut off from the outer world, lie weakly in bed, drinking cup-a-soups and watching my skin turn brown. The news is already on TV; I know what's happening to my body but I do not report it. As I lie in bed, treasuring every breath, I stare at the empty pillow next to mine and wish there was someone beside me. But it is too late for wishes. I put my hand on my heart and realise it has already stopped beating.

When I am lonely for boys what I miss is their bodies. The smell of their skin, its saltiness. The rough whisper of stubble against my cheek. The strong firm hands, the way they rest on the curve of my back.

Eventually my loneliness is strong enough to pull me out of bed. I can smell him lingering on my pillow. The tantalising thread of his scent drags me to the front door and to the streets outside.

I'll find him, one day. And he'll make me remember what it's like to be alive.

ARKADY, KAIN & ZOMBIES

Somewhere between his sixth and seventh drink, Kain forgot what he was doing at the bar.

He lifted his head up off of the table and took in his low-lit surroundings, squinting through the haze of alcohol. Two—no, three—exits. Two men drinking alone to his right, too far gone into their booze to be a threat. Three tables over was a group of women in their mid-thirties. He didn't remember their arrival and the realisation put him on edge, made him wonder what else he'd missed.

"Some counterspy I am," he muttered, shifting slightly in his seat, making sure his back was firmly against the wall. Years of training ensured that there was enough space on his right for another person to squeeze in, although there was no one to protect now, not anymore.

Kain studied the bar patrons more carefully, realised nearly everyone was wearing dark clothing. Even the music was muted, and the furniture was sombre, all of the room's colour silenced. The only spot of brightness was a strip of yellow quarantine police tape along one wall that a waiter was struggling to remove.

He could leave the country, Kain realised, all of a

sudden. The quarantine had been lifted that morning. He could visit London, go back to the old haunts where he and the Russian Ambassador had spent so much time during the Cold War. But for what? All that was left were memories.

Kain shook his head, wished himself back in time for a brief, desperate moment. But he was too practical to harbour that thought for long, so he let his shoulders slump and lifted a hand to order another drink.

That's when he heard it: a low, deep groan that sent shivers down his spine. Kain stiffened, pulled out his gun. There! One of the men on his right groaned a second time, slamming his drink down onto the table. The man had dark hair, and his head was tilted downwards, his features hidden from sight. Slow and uncoordinated movements, broken and dirty fingernails… The man was clearly undead.

A jolt of adrenaline cleared Kain's head. There was no time to waste. He stood up with renewed purpose, caught the elbow of a passing waiter, then flashed his CIA badge, keeping one eye on the zombie.

"Clear the bar," he instructed.

The waiter looked at him, then at the gun in his hand. He had the slightly vacant expression of an inbred sheep. "There's no need to be aggressive, sir. I can get you another drink on the ho—"

"Clear the bar," Kain snapped. "Unless you want to be eaten by a zombie." He shoved the waiter behind him, began to march towards his target.

"But sir!" the waiter said, running after him. "Please! Two free drinks on the house! No, three!" He skidded to a halt in front of Kain, holding his hands up pleadingly.

Kain elbowed him aside. "Get out of my way or you're dead meat." He aimed for the back of the zombie's head.

The waiter stepped in front of Kain, blocking his view. "I see what you did there. Funny, although perhaps too soon after the quarantine to be making jokes?" The idiot placed his hands on Kain's shoulders, tried to steer him back to the other end of the bar. "Now if you'll just sit down…"

Kain shoved the waiter to the ground, lifted his gun again but the zombie was gone. He scanned the bar, alert. There, by the group of women! The zombie was almost upon them, shuffling forward with his head bowed. Kain aimed again, but as he squeezed on the trigger, the waiter reappeared and knocked the gun from his hand. The bullet went wide, shattering a bottle of Screech behind the bar.

Everyone screamed and ducked, until Kain and the waiter were the only ones left standing. He pushed the waiter away again and rolled up his sleeves to deal with the problem the old-fashioned way.

The zombie, like all the other bar patrons, was crouched down on the floor with his head between his hands. So he had learned to mimic human behaviour— the damn things kept getting smarter.

Kain grabbed the zombie by the collar and pulled him upright, landing a punch right on the sucker's nose. He wound his arm back for another punch, then noticed the blood trickling down the zombie's face. Blood.

"What the fuck, man?" the zombie spat, except he wasn't a zombie. He was human.

"I…" Kain paused, let go. All of a sudden the past

twelve months weighed heavily on his shoulders, leaving him old and tired. How could he have made such a serious mistake?

The man wiped his nose on his sleeve, leaving a dark streak across the grey material. He glared at Kain, swaying on his feet. "You wanna fight?" His attempt to look menacing was laughable.

The waiter caught up with them, brushing off his apron. He stepped between Kain and the man, his smile overly wide. "How about no one fights? That sounds good to me." When no one moved, he turned to the man. "Now, you, sir, if you can just come with me to the bathroom, we can get that blood cleaned right off."

When the waiter returned, Kain was still standing in the same spot, staring down at the drops of blood on the floor.

The waiter hesitated, then examined Kain's expression and deemed it safe to approach. "Easy mistake to make, sir. Don't you worry about it. You police people had it harder than most during the quarantine." He pushed Kain over to an empty table, shoved a drink into his hand. "Just sit yourself down and drink up. You'll feel better in no time, okay? Okay." He wandered off to soothe the other patrons.

Kain sat down slowly. Clutched in his fist was a glass of alcohol with a cocktail umbrella in it. He took a sip, realised it was vodka rather than his usual scotch. The umbrella was a bright green colour that reminded him of someone. Ah, yes: Arkady. Where was she again?

*   *   *

One year earlier
"You can't keep me locked up in here forever, you

know." Arkady posed against her bedroom doorway, wearing skimpy jean shorts and a low-cut green t-shirt that ended just above her navel. Her diamond encrusted sunglasses were perched on her head, and—judging by the stilettos she was wearing—she had come up with yet another plan to escape his clutches.

Kain placed his newspaper down on the table, folded into neat quarters. "I'm your counterspy. It's my job to keep track of you and stop you from communicating with other UFIT terrorists. We've already established this."

"And we've already established that I'm not a terrorist, I'm a celebrity." She lengthened the word as if he were too stupid to understand: "Suh-leh-bri-tea."

"A celebrity who happens to be the spokesperson for a terrorist organisation," Kain replied, keeping his comments on the wisdom of said terrorist group to himself. He picked up his marker and went back to censoring the newspaper. Years spent working for the CIA, controlling the flow of intelligence, and now here he was near the end of his career, babysitting a spoilt brat.

Arkady slinked closer, trailing a hand up Kain's arm. "Such muscles," she purred, moving her fingers to trail along his collarbone. Kain worked his jaw but did not move. Her hand trailed across to his other shoulder as she circled to stand behind him. Then her lips were beside his ear. "I've always liked older men."

"I still won't let you leave the house," he replied flatly.

She sighed, and her hot breath sent shivers down his spine. Her hand slipped down from his shoulder to his chest.

Kain swallowed. "Ms Denver, if you don't stop this instant I'll—"

A finger against his lips. "You'll what? Tie me up again?" she drawled, her Texas twang growing stronger. She ran the tip of her tongue along his earlobe and breathed, "Kinky."

"That's it!" Kain jumped to his feet, grabbed Arkady and shoved her into a chair. "If you're not going to cooperate, we'll have to do this the hard way."

Arkady lounged back, her bright green t-shirt stretching enticingly. "Hard? I like it hard."

"Fine," Kain snapped, more angry at himself for letting her get to him. He stormed off to the kitchen and returned with a roll of duct tape, then dropped to his knees and bound Arkady's legs to the chair before she could react.

"Hey!" She tried to hit him but he grabbed her hands and taped them together too. He stood back to admire his handiwork, then frowned: something was missing. "This is so not cool," Arkady complained, waving her hands. "What is it with you and duct tape anyway?"

Kain broke off a small piece of tape with his teeth and covered Arkady's mouth. "Better," he said, nodding in satisfaction. Now he could think.

He took a moment to enjoy the silence, then eyed Arkady's clothing with growing disapproval. She only ever wore that ridiculous outfit when she was off to one of her TV interviews. No doubt she'd been communicating with UFIT behind his back, planning another unapproved excursion.

Kain straightened. "This is how it's going to work: I ask the questions, you answer the questions.

Understood?"

Arkady nodded, her eyebrows drawn together in a childlike scowl. That this woman was of so much apparent importance never failed to amaze him.

He pulled the tape off of her mouth. "Who are you meeting today?"

"No one. I was only—"

Kain smoothed the tape firmly over her lips again, muffling any sound. Arkady's eyes flared with indignation but he remained unmoved. "*I* ask the questions. You answer them. Nothing else. Got it?"

She nodded a second time, now more resigned.

"Where are you going?" Kain asked, then pulled off the tape.

Arkady tilted her head to one side and fluttered her eyelashes. "Why, Kainy? Would you miss me?" This time when Kain resealed her lips she began humming *The Song That Doesn't End*.

Kain ignored her, moving to sit at the table. When Arkady began humming even louder he took his newspaper, shook it out, and began reading.

Five choruses of *The Song That Doesn't End* later, Arkady had tired of humming and had resorted to rocking back and forth on her chair, banging the chair legs down on the floor with each swing. The newspaper shook in Kain's hands, but he forced himself to remain patient. He needed this job, could not afford to mess it up. The money, he thought. Think about the money.

Eventually Arkady quietened and glared sullenly at Kain. He took his time, finished censoring the last article in the newspaper—a sensationalist piece warning of an impending epidemic. It was only then that Kain stood up to remove the gag.

"Are you ready to talk?" he asked.

Arkady pouted, looked away. "Only if you leave the tape off."

"Then answer my questions."

"I told you," she said, wiggling her toes. "I'm not going anywhere. Now untie me, Kainy."

He wasn't going to get anything else from her, at least not like this. Kain grabbed a pair of scissors and kneeled down to cut through the duct tape, ready to spring into action if Arkady so much as looked toward the front door. But she just sat there, docile, watching him with a curious expression on her face, somewhere between amusement and affection.

"Thanks," she said when he was done. She leaned forward, tilted his chin towards her. "You wanna know why I dressed up?" she asked softly. She didn't wait for him to reply. "A girl gets locked up in a house by a big, strong man like you, with no phones, no internet, no TV, nothing to do… Well, it gets a little lonely, you see?"

Kain froze, every alarm bell in his head going off. He was a counterspy, he was a professional. He couldn't get attached to his target: it wasn't allowed. Already his friendship with the Ambassador in his previous mission had run too deep, and now this… This…

The doorbell rang.

Arkady bounced to her feet. "That'll be my boyfriend!" She raced over to the front door, then paused and glanced back at Kain, still kneeling on the floor. "Oh Kainy," she said with a cruel smile, "You didn't think I meant *you*, did you, darling?"

She opened the front door before he could react, throwing herself into her boyfriend's arms. "I've missed you, Chandler," she said, planting a long, lingering kiss on his lips.

Kain gritted his teeth and got to his feet. He had only met Chandler one time before, and the memory of that evening still gave him a migraine. Chandler was a male model and the epitome of stupid, if stupid had large bleached-white teeth and skin two shades past a natural tan.

"Chandler? Babe, what's wrong?"

When Arkady stepped away, Chandler did not follow. Kain moved closer, one hand drifting to his gun. Chandler stood there in a half-daze, as if under a considerable amount of anaesthetic. His pupils were dilated and his every breath came in slow, laboured pants.

"I…" Chandler cleared his throat, started again. "I…" He held up his hand. A ring of teeth marks circled his palm, bruising his skin like an apple three days too old, all mushy purples and reds.

"Oh honey!" Arkady exclaimed, taking his hand. "What happened?"

Thankfully Kain's cell phone began to ring, giving him an excuse to turn his back on the couple. He pulled the phone out of his suit pocket, glanced at the number. It was Everett, his boss. Kain put the phone to his ear and answered: "Sir?"

"Kain. Secure Ms Denver on the rooftop. Shoot anyone who approaches. I repeat: shoot anyone who approaches." There was a strained edge to Everett's voice that Kain had never heard before. "We're trying to secure a private helicopter for you, but if you come into contact with anyone we won't be allowed to evacuate you."

"Sir?"

"The epidemic, Kain," Everett said impatiently. "Haven't you read the papers?"

Everett had fallen for that ridiculous article? Kain opened his mouth, then wondered whether it was just another UFIT stunt, as every increase in Arkady's celebrity status helped push terrorism into the mainstream. Sex really could sell anything. Kain sighed. "Yes, sir. Right away, sir." The words were barely out of his mouth before the line went dead.

He had his orders; all he could do was follow them. Kain slipped his phone back into his suit pocket, then turned around to give Arkady the news. She was still crooning over Chandler's hand, leaning forward far enough that her tiny shorts had ridden up her leg.

"Say goodbye to Chandler, Ms Denver," he said, retrieving a bag of emergency rations from the kitchen. "We need to go."

"You bet we do." She put her hands on her hips. "We need to take Chandler to a hospital." When Kain didn't react, she pointed straight at Chandler's unresponsive face. "Look at him, K! He needs help!"

"I don't care," Kain replied. He quickly rifled through the day's newspapers, searching for the elusive epidemic article. There! Best to read the article later and gather intelligence on the supposed 'epidemic'.

"You never care about anyone." Arkady's eyes blazed with the righteousness of youth and for a moment Kain was tempted to tell her that no, no one mattered, because at the end of the day everyone was just a job and sooner or later they'd be gone forever. But he held his tongue.

"My priority is your safety," he said instead. "Now

come on."

Just then Chandler's legs gave out beneath him and he collapsed to the ground, spasming, his face turning red, his eyes bulging out of their sockets. His groan was strangled, more a grunt than a cry, deep and low like the snorting of a pig. Arkady crouched down, trying to pin one of Chandler's flailing arms, but was knocked away almost immediately, her sunglasses skittering across the floor.

Then the seizure was over, and Chandler did not move again. Froth bubbled at his lips, tinged with blood. A shiver of premonition went down Kain's spine.

Arkady had a hand over her mouth. Her legs trembled as she stood. "Is he…?"

Kain squatted to take Chandler's pulse. Nothing. He pulled back Chandler's eyelids, noticed the unnatural milkiness of the pupils. Kain tried to move an arm but it was stiff and heavy. Rigor mortis had already set in even though Chandler could not have been dead for more than a few minutes.

How was this possible? He looked over the newspaper article, read through it again, cross-referencing the symptoms. Every single one matched. All of a sudden Kain found himself wishing he hadn't censored some of the words in case they contained crucial information. Everett hadn't been joking: the epidemic was real.

Now it was even more of a priority to accompany Arkady to the roof. Kain looked up at his target, found her eyes full of tears. He stood, uncomfortable. "He's dead," Kain confirmed unnecessarily, because he didn't know what else to say. A solitary tear clung persistently to the tip of Arkady's nose, as if it could not bear to leave her.

Arkady wiped her face, blinked, wiped her face again. "That's convenient," she said brightly, her smile as brittle as newly-formed frost. "Now you don't need to throw him out." She took a deep breath. "So where were we going again?"

"The roof," he replied, taking her by the elbow and steering her into the hallway outside. He closed the front door behind him for good measure; better that Everett never found out they'd been in contact with someone infected.

Arkady was going into shock. Kain rubbed her arms awkwardly, found himself wondering yet again how she had ended up the spokesperson for a terrorist group. Had she even seen a dead body before?

"Say Kainy," Arkady said, moving close enough to lean her head on his shoulder. Her voice sounded off, dreamy, as if her mind were somewhere far, far away from the dead body on the other side of the door. "You know your old target, the Ambassador guy you guarded before me? He was a really old geezer. So I was wondering… When was the last time you've had sex?"

Kain shrugged her off of his shoulder. "That is none of your concern," he said stiffly. There was no room for jokes in an emergency.

"You can't be a celibate loner *forever*." He gave her a look and she huffed irritably. "I guess if anyone could, you can. But that's no fun!"

"My job isn't to have fun."

Arkady stuck out her bottom lip. "Live a little. Just this once?"

Their eyes touched for a moment too long. Kain

looked away first. "Come on, let's get you to the roof."

"Wait! My sunglasses! I'm photosensitive, you know. I can't go anywhere without them." She looked at the front door, hesitated. "They're in the flat…"

Against his better judgement, Kain relented. "I'll get them."

He pulled open the front door to find Chandler standing on the other side. His face was pale, his eyes open but unseeing, a thick white film covering the pupils. Saliva still bubbled at his lips, the drool sliding down his stubbled chin.

"Chandler?" Arkady stepped forward, relieved. "I thought you were dead! He said you were dead!" She looked at Kain, eyes narrowed. "You *said* he was dead!"

Chandler didn't reply. He reached out, grabbed Arkady's arm and pulled her to him. Then he sank his teeth into her shoulder, into the soft spot beneath her neck.

Arkady screamed.

Kain burst into motion, punching Chandler's nose at a forty-five degree angle so that the nasal bone would snap and push upwards into the brain. The force sent Chandler's head upwards and his teeth clicked on empty air but he didn't seem to notice the pain, didn't reel back, dazed, as any normal person would.

Another punch, this time to the underside of the jaw. Then a hand chop to the wrist to free Arkady's arm. Chandler groaned, but it was an involuntary sound with no true feeling, like the creaking of an oak tree in a heavy storm.

Kain pulled Arkady behind him, pulled out his gun and fired. The bullet tore through Chandler's forehead, knocking him to the ground, viscous fluid spraying out of the bullet hole and onto the floor. But not even that stopped Chandler: he reached out, wrapped long, strong fingers around Kain's ankle, dragging him closer, mouth wide open and hungry.

Kain fired twice more, severing Chandler's arm at the wrist. The blood that oozed out was thick and brown, congealed. Still no reaction, no cry of pain. Chandler used his stump to drag himself forward, leaving a trail of slime across the floor. He found his balance, began to push up to his feet.

Kain took careful aim, then fired, fired again, aiming for Chandler's legs, knocking him back into the flat. First the right tibia, then the left, then the other bones until Chandler could but drag himself along the floor. Kain slammed the front door closed and kicked away the dead hand lying at his feet.

"No sunglasses, then," Arkady said, shaken.

Through the wooden door came the sound of scratching, thin and persistent.

"The roof," Kain said, taking Arkady's arm. He didn't let himself think about the bite on Arkady's shoulder, the ring of toothmarks torn into her t-shirt. Had that been enough to transfer the virus? Would Arkady too become like Chandler?

He had failed, Kain realised with sudden sickening dread. Years of training as a counterspy and he had failed to protect his target.

They got to the roof without encountering another person, the hallways quiet. Kain kept his gun in his hand, motioned for Arkady to stay back. He inched through the door and onto the roof, scanned the perimeter, then gave Arkady the all-clear. As she walked outside, shading her eyes with her hand, he barricaded the door.

When he was finished, he joined Arkady at the edge of the roof, staring down at the busy streets below. Commuters marched up and down the pavement on their lunch breaks, oblivious to the impending danger.

"I'm going to die, aren't I?" Arkady said softly. Her hand raised to cover the darkening bite on her shoulder.

Kain hesitated. His silence said it all.

Arkady turned away from the edge of the roof, sliding down to sit cross-legged. She patted the ground beside her, and when Kain sat down stiffly, she scooted closer and laid her head on his shoulder.

Kain pinched the bridge of his nose, one eye firmly on the roof door. Chandler had been bitten en-route to the flat. Extrapolating the data indicated that, assuming Arkady was infected, she had an hour or so left to live. Kain glanced at her face, noted the still and focused expression that told him she was having the same thoughts.

He stretched his legs out in front of him. "Everett is coming to get us. He'll have a cure."

Arkady didn't reply but she slid sideways until she was lying down fully, her head in his lap. Kain didn't have the heart to move her. Their eyes touched, held, the moment stretching out into eternity. When she wasn't talking or being otherwise annoying, she was almost pretty.

Then Arkady sighed loudly and broke the spell. "This stinks," she said. "The bite, I mean. It smells funny."

Infection setting in. Kain half-shrugged, intent on watching the roof door. Had he heard scratching?

"It's probably the most disgusting thing I've seen in my life," Arkady continued, twisting her neck to better study her shoulder. "My first kill is definitely going to be whoever invented this. He could have made dying a lot sexier, you know."

Kain shushed her, strained his ears, hand drifting to his gun. No, the sound was gone now. Perhaps he had imagined it.

She noticed his expression. "What's wrong?"

"Nothing." Everything. Why had Everett sent them to the roof? It was a death trap; there were no alternative escape routes.

From the streets below came several screams, blaring car horns. Kain stiffened, Arkady said nothing. Her eyes were beginning to lose focus and she was breathing heavily, as if in pain. The ugly truth of the festering wound on her shoulder was impossible to ignore and Kain wondered which would come first: her death, or monsters pushing their way through the door.

Twenty minutes later his phone rang, and Kain answered in relief. "Sir. We're on the roof."

"Kain." Everett sighed. "I'm sorry, Kain. We're not coming."

"Sir?"

"The entire city is under quarantine. There's nothing I can do. Any helicopter that picks up passengers will be shot down."

Kain looked down at Arkady's face, so open and vulnerable in his lap. She smiled, twined her fingers through his. Her face was pale and there was a faint sheen of perspiration across her forehead; her shoulder was a study of bruises, the skin blued and purpled and swollen, sickly.

"Sounds great, sir," he said. He checked his watch. She had about half an hour left.

"What are you talking about, Kain?"

"I'll see you soon." He hung up before Everett could reply, then surreptitiously turned his phone off. He slid it into his suit pocket.

"They're coming?" Arkady asked weakly. She tried to lift her head to look at the skyline but her neck was too weak to support the weight.

Kain slid an arm under her neck, careful to avoid her injured shoulder. "Of course," he told her, propping up her head. "Everett's sending a helicopter. They'll cure you."

"They better." Her eyes drifted closed, then opened again. "I'm a celebrity, you know."

"I know," Kain replied, and when she closed her eyes again, he sat there quietly and held her close, and watched the empty skies.

*   *   *

"Sir? Sir? We're closing." A hand touched his shoulder.

Kain jolted, grabbed the man by the shirt collar and slammed him onto the tabletop. His heart was racing and his hand reached for a gun that was... That was missing.

The surprise pulled him up short. Kain realised where he was, let go of the waiter's shirt and stepped back. The bar was empty, the bar stools packed up on top of the counter and the dim mood lighting replaced by a harsh glare. The room smelled faintly of bleach, and beneath that was the ever-present sharp bar tang of spilled beer.

"The exit's that way," the waiter said, smoothing down his top. "And I've left your gun on the table beside the door. Took it for safe-keeping, you see."

Kain didn't reply. He marched over to the exit, slipped his gun into its holster, then pushed through the door and into the evening air. He looked up and down the street to get his bearings, then headed left because the path looked familiar.

When he turned the corner, Kain stopped in his tracks. Across the street was a cemetery.

The gates were still open. Kain scanned his surroundings for potential threats, then crossed the road and went into the cemetery. Inside was a mass of steel and concrete graves, each roughly etched with a skull-and-crossbones. There were no names nor dates nor loving messages on the gravestones, nothing at all to tell one apart from the other, just long rows of blank faces in the gloom.

In the very centre of the cemetery was a large grey plinth inscribed with hundreds of names. This too was familiar.

Kain circled the plinth, felt a shiver settle over his shoulders. When he put his hands in his pockets, his fingers touched something unfamiliar: a bright green cocktail umbrella. The colour reminded him of someone.

He circled the plinth again, stopped to stare at the one square inch that looked the most familiar. His fingers traced the contours of that name and then he crouched down to push the cocktail umbrella into the soft dirt beneath.

Kain bowed his head. A solitary tear tracked its way

across his cheek, clinging to the very tip of his nose as if it could not bear to leave him.

ELECTRICITY

She
waited in
the darkness
for the lights
to come back
on, watching
the steady
burning of
candles.

Her feet were numb, her heart
thudded loudly in her ears, and as
the minutes passed the candles
burned lower and the darkness
thickened. Eventually it dawned on
her that he was never coming back.
It was only then that she allowed
the first tears of mourning to fall,
big fat drops that trickled down her
cheeks like softly melted wax. Later
she would tell the neighbours that
the zombies had gotten him on his
way to the basement, had torn him
apart and feasted on his brains. And
only she would know the truth: he
had broken the love between them,
and left her behind in the darkness.

AFTERWORD

I'll let you in on a secret: I hate zombies.

It's not just that they're diseased and decaying, even though I am terribly squeamish (the bit in *The Perfect Song* where Michael's nail rips off still makes me shudder); what really frightens me about zombies is their mindless persistence and hunger. Zombies are overwhelming, irrational, unstoppable. You cannot defend yourself against them. And if you step back and think of zombies that way, well they're not so different from love, then, are they?

Now, credit where credit is due: I didn't think of this zombie love theme all by myself. I have Mari Juniper, Lori Titus, Jim Bronyaur and Jodi MacArthur to thank for organising the Zombie Luv Flash Fiction Contest, which was hosted over on *Mari's Randomities* the summer of 2010. I wrote *Promises* overnight, and then my mind was stuck in the zombie gutter.

A number of people have asked me how I can keep writing stories on the same theme, and the simple answer is that my creativity works best in small spaces. The longer answer probably includes the words 'insane' and 'desperate coffee drinking'.

Some of the stories in this collection are edited, extended or otherwise mutated versions of #fridayflash stories of mine, including *Swimming Lessons*, *A Prayer* to *Garlic*, and several parts of *Seven Birds*. *The Perfect Song* was originally published in The Random Eye magazine (defunct), now appearing in a zombie-tweaked version. Others were written exclusively for this collection, such as *Hungry for You* and *Dead Man's Rose*, two of my favourites. And of course *Arkady, Kain & Zombies* would not have existed if not for MCM, author and creator of *Arkady & Kain*, who kindly lent me his characters.

Something that entertained me whilst writing this collection was the (hopefully) sneaky use of hidden messages. *Electricity* is an anagram of my sister's name. *Seven Birds*—inspired by the 12 Days of Christmas—only has six parts instead of the expected seven, because the relationship ends before expected. In *Dead Man's Rose,* the number '6' is repeated three times to suggest hell, there are several rose references (alba, bourbon), a rose over a doorway indicating secrets (sub rosa), and other silly little details. Every story, however short, has a unique history.

But the one thing all the stories in this collection share is that they were specially put together for you.

That's right, *you*.

So if you have any burning questions or comments or thoughts, do drop me a line at http://amharte.com.

Especially if you know a good zombie joke.

ACKNOWLEDGEMENTS

This collection would not have been possible without the inspiration and encouragement of a number of people. My thanks in particular to Constella Espj, Merrilee Faber, Sheila Lathia, MCM, and the wonderful Qazyfiction fans who—for reasons unknown—keep subjecting themselves to my stories.

About the Author

A.M. Harte is a London-based speculative fiction enthusiast and chocolate addict. She's a writer, practical joker, and an advocate of indie publishing in any shape or form. She is excellent at missing deadlines, has long forgotten what 'free time' means, and enjoys procrastinating far too much.

To find out more, please visit http://amharte.com.

MORE FROM 1889 LABS

Kidney Disease Gave Me Brain Damage

What do bunny tacos, sonic toothbrushes, the AntiChrist and angry gnomes have in common? More than you can imagine, dear reader. More than you can possibly want to imagine.

The Antithesis

Heaven and Hell like you've never seen them before. New Jury recruit Alezair Czynri lives in Purgatory and helps enforce the Code between angels and demons. But a storm lays just over the horizon… one that brings with it a war.

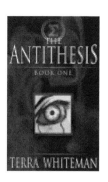

Intern With A Vampire

Human medicine is easy. On her first day at Grace General Hospital, new intern Aline Harman risks vampire infection, demonic possession, and having her heart torn out of her chest… and this from her colleagues.

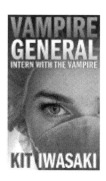

Ventricle, Atrium

Gabriel Gadfly's much anticipated second anthology is a vivid and tender tribute to the life cycle of love — the sex, the laughter, the pain, the sweetness, the fear, the vacancy.

Gangster

From the dark, basement speakeasies of 1926 Chicago, to the decadent parties of the Hollywood elite, psychopathic Clara slices her way through various people across America in her quest for fame.

1889 Labs is an independent publisher dedicated to producing the best strange fiction conceivable by the human brain. Catering to a specific demographic of men and women between the ages of 3 and 97, we print everything from kids books to serious stories for adults. Our goal is to bring you on an amazing adventure onscreen and off. We hope you'll take us up on the offer.

For more information and our full list of books, visit http://1889.ca

IMPOSSIBLE ODDS

from "Kidney Disease Gave Me Brain Damage
by MCM

Ten minutes into the meeting, Jacob finished with pleasantries and took to the whiteboards. With confident strokes, he sketched "PUBLICITY" across the entire length of the wall.

"So," he said, clicking the pen closed with a smile. "Let's break it down for you."

Sara, Anna and Gretchen said nothing, just stared expectantly. Jacob winked at Sara, and she blushed, giving him the juice he needed to roll.

"Publicity is not as hard as you think," he said, starting his trademark stroll across the room. "Publicity is about connecting with your customers, about—"

"Sorry, Jacob," said Anna suddenly. "Can I interrupt you for a second?"

Jacob didn't miss a beat. He nodded broadly and motioned as if he were indeed handing the meeting over to her. "Absolutely!" he said jovially. "Let's do it!"

She took a pocket projector from her bag and turned it on. Instantly, an image appeared on the wall beside them: a complex graph of detailed demographics, broken down by market segment and sexual preference.

"We want to take things in a new direction," she said. "After internal discussion, we realised we need to be a little more cutting-edge with our plans."

"Exactly where I want you to be," he smiled. "You read my mind."

"What we want to do is show how people relate to our product in an intimate way. We feel like we're being too clinical."

She clicked her laptop and the image changed to show a woman with an iPhone pressed up against her naked breast.

"Hold on," said Jacob, trying not to laugh. "We're still talking about accounting software, right?"

"Yes," Anna said seriously.

"Okay," said Jacob. "I… um… so we're saying keeping track of cash flow is a lot like… um… a baby latched on to her nipple."

"Yes."

"I see," said Jacob. "I see, and I like it! It's unorthodox, and very cutting edge! 'Strange Publicity' is where it's at. Are you sure you've never done this before?"

He winked at Sara again, and kept up the seamless, confident act for another fifty minutes, until the three women bustled off to their next appointment, leaving him in a room of what amounted to gadget porn. When Rick came in, he hadn't moved an inch.

"Gavelston's calling for you," Rick said, staring at the glossy print-outs on the table. "She said you didn't file proper expense reports for… uh… what's all this?"

"Long story," Jacob sighed. "Gonna be a long week, too."

"Looks like it. Need any help?"

"Nah," said Jacob, snapping back to attention. "I've got this under control."

* * *

Seven days and ten hours of sleep later, Jacob had the whiteboards covered with mock-ups. Women with iPhones on breasts, sleeping next to Blackberries, caressing a Palm Pre. It was intimate and sensual and he couldn't stand to look at it anymore.

"Good morning, ladies," he said as they took their seats. "I think you're going to like what I have to show you today."

Anna leaned back in her chair, browsed the options, and glanced over at Gretchen, who nodded back.

"Actually," she said, "we've done some internal testing."

Jacob's arms dropped to his sides. "You have," he said without knowing how he felt.

"Yes," Anna continued, "and what we found is that the porn motif you seem to have embraced, it just doesn't sit well with our customers. They feel exploited. Used. And it's not the kind of image we're trying to project."

Jacob's mouth was hanging open, but he closed it quickly, smiled, nodding. "Absolutely," he said. "You're so right. Businesswomen hate being exploited, and what I've done here? That's just salt on a wound. What *you* need is—"

"Social media," said Anna. "Viral marketing."

"Exactly!" laughed Jacob, snapping his fingers for effect. "Exactly! Viral marketing, like—"

"Something outrageous."

"Yes, like—"

"How to make a male body part cake."

Jacob's smile barely faltered, but he had run out of things to say. He looked from Anna to Gretchen, and from Gretchen to Sara. Sara was blushing, but the other two were dead serious.

"Male… body part… cake."

"Yes."

"Okay. And by male body part, you mean…"

"Yes."

"Okay."

"It needs to be easy for people to make," said Anna, "and be as accurate as possible, so that they feel a sense of accomplishment. You can handle the rest, yes?"

Jacob laughed, but caught himself, waved it off. "Oh yeah," he said. "Don't worry about a thing."

"Excellent," said Anna, at the door. "We'll see you Friday, then? We're really excited about this new direction, Jacob. We're really looking forward to seeing what you come up with."

They left him in silence, his eyes fixed on a blank paper on the table. It wasn't blank in his mind. Rick popped his head in the door, grinning.

"How'd it go, porno-boy?" Jacob said nothing. There was nothing to say. "We need the room in ten. Can you clear out by then?" Jacob nodded. "And seriously, man. Keep those pics away from Gavelston. She's on the rampage today, and this won't help."

Jacob ran each picture through the shredder, just to be sure.

*   *   *

Jacob almost spilled his coffee when they sat down across from him, polished and elegant, glaring at his dishevelled state. He shuffled his black-covered folders, trying to keep from crying. It had been a long few days.

Sara was the last to enter, her periwinkle peasant skirt drawing Jacob's eyes like a moth to a flame. It was so hypnotic and yet off-putting all at the same time, and when she sat down to face him, he felt himself about to drool.

"I'm really excited about today's meeting," said Anna with a touch of compassion in her voice. "I hope you are, too."

"I am," said Jacob, snapping back to attention, trying to put on his best smile. "It took a lot of doing, but I think I found a really great recipe that will appeal to women of all ages."

He handed the folders over, but before they could open them, the door crept open and Gavelston entered, her greying hair pulled back tight in a bun, her face stretched wide and stern. "Is this a good time?" she asked, and Jacob just about shrieked.

"Oh yes!" said Anna, standing. "Please come in. Jacob is just about to show us his grand creation."

Gavelston looked at Jacob, looked him up and down with visible distaste, and then turned back to Anna with a smile. "I'm as excited as you are," she said.

The four women opened the folders at the same time, and Gretchen let out a gasp, dropped hers. Jacob avoided Gavelston's furious stare, lowering his head into his hands.

"What is *this*?" said Anna, pushing her copy across the table so the cake design was directly under Jacob's face. "Is this some kind of joke?"

Jacob looked up at her, trying to find the words.

"I'm so sorry," said Gavelston, taking the other folders from Sara and Gretchen. "I'm so sorry this happened. Believe me when I say this will be taken care of most severely. *Most* severely."

She sneered at Jacob, snatched his copy away and

threw it in the trash.

"They… they wanted it…" he whimpered, then realised what he'd said, and smacked his head into the table.

"You are *fired*," fumed Gavelston. She touched Gretchen lightly on the shoulder, and motioned to the door. "If you'll come with me, we can find someone better suited to your needs."

The two of them left as Anna and Sara stood, avoiding eye contact with Jacob as he disintegrated into tears and coffee stains.

"You… you asked for it, didn't you?" he sobbed. "I heard you. You asked for it."

"Oh, Jacob," said Anna. "We didn't ask for it. *You* asked for it, the second you broke Marie's heart."

Jacob looked up, eyes wide. "M-M-Marie?"

"You think you can cheat and get away with it, Mr Big Shot? Think again. You may not care about anyone but yourself, but *we do*. We asked her what would help her, and you know what she said?"

Jacob shook his head slowly.

"Inflicting pain to Jacob," Anna beamed. "How you feeling now, Mr Big Shot?"

Jacob sighed, rested his head against the table. Anna left the room with a bounce in her step, but Sara came around beside him, crouched down and rested a hand on his shoulder.

"I'm sorry," she said softly. "But I don't date unemployed men. See you around!"

Jacob was removed by security ten minutes later.

Printed in Poland
by Amazon Fulfillment
Poland Sp. z o.o., Wrocław

49536953R00082